FRANK ON THE LOWER MISSISSIPPI

HARRY CASTLEMON

Frank on the Lower Mississippi

Harry Castlemon

© 1st World Library – Literary Society, 2006
PO Box 2211
Fairfield, IA 52556
www.1stworldlibrary.org
First Edition

LCCN: 2006905708

Softcover ISBN: 1-4218-2137-0
Hardcover ISBN: 1-4218-2037-4
eBook ISBN: 1-4218-2237-7

Purchase *"Frank on the Lower Mississippi"*
as a traditional bound book at:
www.1stWorldLibrary.org/purchase.asp?ISBN=1-4218-2137-0

1st World Library Literary Society is a nonprofit
organization dedicated to promoting literacy by:

- Creating a free internet library accessible from any computer worldwide.
- Hosting writing competitions and offering book publishing scholarships.

Readers interested in supporting literacy
through sponsorship, donations or
membership please contact:
literacy@1stworldlibrary.org
Check us out at: www.1stworldlibrary.ORG
and start downloading free ebooks today.

CONTENTS

CHAPTER I

THE NEW PAYMASTER

Vicksburg had fallen, and the army had marched in and taken possession of the city. How Frank longed to accompany it, that he might see the inside of the rebel stronghold, which had so long withstood the advance of our fleet and army! He stood leaning against one of the monster guns, which, at his bidding, had spoken so often and so effectively in favor of the Union, and for two hours watched the long lines of war-worn soldiers as they moved into the works. At length a tremendous cheer arose from the city, and Frank discovered a party of soldiers on the cupola of the court-house, from which, a few moments afterward, floated the Stars and Stripes. Then came faintly to his ears the words of a familiar song, which were caught up by the soldiers in the city, then by those who were still marching in, and "We'll rally round the flag, boys," was sung by an immense choir. The rebels in the streets gazed wonderingly at the men on the spire, and listened to the song, and the triumphant shouts of the conquering army, which proclaimed the beginning of the downfall of their confederacy.

To Frank, it was one of the proudest moments of his life - a sight he would not have missed to be able to float at the mast-head of his vessel the broad pennant of the admiral. All he had endured was forgotten; and when the Old Flag was unfurled in the air which had but a short time before floated the "stars and bars," he pulled off his cap and shouted at the top of his lungs.

Having thus given vent to his feelings of exultation, in obedience to orders, he commenced the removal of his battery on board the Trenton. It was two days' work to accomplish this, but Frank, who was impatient to see the inside of the fortifications worked with a will, and finally the battery was mounted in its old position. On the following day, the Trenton moved down the river, and came to anchor in front of Vicksburg. Shore liberty was granted, and Frank, in company with several of his brother officers, strolled about the city. On every side the houses bore the marks of Union shot and shell, and the streets were blocked with fortifications, showing that had the city been taken by storm, it was the intention of the rebels to dispute every inch of the ground. Every thing bore evidence to the fact that the fight had been a most desperate one; that the rebels had surrendered only when they found that it was impossible to hold out longer.

In some places the streets ran through deep cuts in the bank, and in these banks were the famous "gopher holes." They were [ca]ves dug in the ground, into which a person, if he happened to hear a shell coming, might run for safety. Outside the city, the fortifications were most extensive; rifle-pits ran in every direction, flanked by strong forts, whose battered walls attested the fury of the iron hail that had been poured upon them. It was night before Frank was aware of it, so interested was he in every thing about him, and he returned on board his vessel, weary with his long walk, but amply repaid by seeing the inside of what its rebel occupants had called "the Gibraltar of America."

During the next two days, several vessels of the squadron passed the city, on their way to new fields of action further down the river. One of them - the Boxer, a tin-clad, mounting eight guns - had Frank on board. He had been detached from the Trenton, and ordered to join this vessel, which had been assigned a station a short distance below Grand Gulf. As usual, he had no difficulty in becoming acquainted with his new messmates, and he soon felt perfectly at home among them. He found, as he had done in every other mess of which he had

Harry Castlemon

been a member, that there was the usual amount of wrangling and disputing, and it amused him exceedingly. All the mess seemed to be indignant at the caterer, who did not appear to stand very high in their estimation. The latter, he learned, had just made an "assessment" upon the mess to the amount of ten dollars for each member; and as there was no paymaster on board, the officers had but very little ready money, and were anxious to know where all the funds paid into the treasury went to. He also found that the caterer's authority was not as much respected as he had a right to claim, for during the very first meal Frank ate in the mess, a dispute arose which threatened for a time to end in the whole matter being carried before the captain.

One of the members of the mess, who was temporarily attached to the vessel, was a pilot who had been pressed into the service. He was a genuine rebel, and frequently said that he was called a traitor because he was in favor of allowing the South to "peaceably withdraw from the Union." The doctor, a little, fat, jolly man, and a thorough Unionist, who believed in handling all rebels without gloves, took up the sword, and the debate that followed was long and stormy. The pilot, as it proved, hardly knew the reasons why the South had attempted to secede, and was constantly clinching his arguments by saying, "Men who know more, and who have done more fighting during this war than you, Doctor Brown, say that they have a right to do so." The debate waxed hotter and hotter, until some of the other members of the mess joined in with the doctor against the pilot, and the caterer, thinking that the noise the disputants made was unbecoming the members of a well-regulated mess, at length shouted:

"Silence! Gentlemen, hereafter talking politics in this wardroom is strictly prohibited."

"Eh?" ejaculated the doctor, who was thoroughly aroused, "Do you expect us to sit here and listen to a conscript running down the Government - a man who never would have entered the service if he had not been compelled to do so? No, sir! I wouldn't hold my tongue under such circumstances if all the six-foot-four caterers in the squadron should say so. You are not a little admiral, to come down here and hoist your broad pennant in this mess-room."

The caterer was astounded when he found his authority thus set at defiance, and without further parley he retired to his room; and in a few moments returned with the books, papers, and the small amount of money that belonged to the mess; laying them on the table, he said:

"Gentlemen, you will please elect another caterer."

The debate was instantly hushed, for not one member of the mess, besides the caterer just resigned, could have been hired to take the responsibility of managing affairs. When the officers had finished their dinner, they walked carelessly out on deck, as if the question of where the next meal was to come from did not trouble them in the least. Nothing was done toward an election; no one took charge of the books or papers, and when the table was cleared away they were thrown unceremoniously under the water-cooler. The money, however, was taken care of by the doctor. Dinner-time came, and when Frank, tired and hungry, was relieved from the deck, he inquired what was to be had to eat.

"There's nothing been done about it yet," answered the officer who relieved him. "The steward went to several of the members of the mess, and asked what they wished served up; but they told him that they had nothing to do with the caterer's business, and the consequence is, if you want any thing to eat, you will have to go into the pantry and help yourself."

Frank was a good deal amused at the obstinacy displayed by the different members of the mess, and wondered how the affair would end. The mess could not long exist without some one to take charge of it; but for himself he was not at all concerned. He had paid no initiation fee, because no one had asked him for it, and he knew that as long as there were provisions in the paymaster's store-rooms, there was no danger but that he would get plenty to eat. He found three or four officers in the pantry making their dinner on hard-tack, pickles, and raw bacon. They were all grumbling over the hard fare, but not one of them appeared willing to assume the office of caterer.

Things went on in this way for nearly a week, (during which time they had arrived at their station,) and the doctor, who was fond of good living, could stand it no longer. He went to the caterer who had resigned, and, after considerable urging, and a solemn promise that politics should not again be discussed in the mess, the latter was persuaded to resume the management of affairs. The change from hard crackers and pickles to nice warm meals was a most agreeable one, and the jolly doctor, according to promise, was very careful what questions were brought up before the mess for discussion.

By this time, as we have before remarked, the Boxer had arrived at her station. Her crew thought they were now about to lead a life of idleness and inactivity, for not a rebel had they seen since leaving Vicksburg. But one morning, while the men were engaged in washing off the forecastle, they were startled by a roar of musketry, and three of the sailors fell dead upon the deck.

The fight that followed continued for two hours, the rebels finally retiring, not because they had been worsted, but for the reason that they had grown weary of the engagement. This was the commencement of a series of attacks which proved to be the source of great annoyance to the crew of the Boxer. The guerrillas would appear when least expected, and the levee afforded them a secure hiding-place from which they could not be driven, either with big guns or small arms. They were fatal marksmen, too; and during the week following, the Boxer's crew lost ten men. One rebel in particular attracted their attention, and his reckless courage excited their admiration. He rode a large white horse, and although rendered a prominent mark for the rifles of the sailors, he always escaped unhurt. He would ride boldly out in full view of the vessel, patiently wait for someone to expose himself, when the sharp crack of his rifle would be followed by the report made to the captain, "A man shot, sir."

Frank had selected this man as a worthy foe-man; and every time he appeared the young officer was on the watch for him. He was very expert with the rifle, and after a few shots, he succeeded in convincing the rebel that the safest place for him was behind the levee. One morning the foe appeared in stronger force than usual, and conspicuous among them was the white horse and his daring rider. The fight that ensued had continued for perhaps half an hour, when the quartermaster reported the dispatch-boat approaching. As soon as she came within range, the guerrillas directed their fire against her, to which the latter replied briskly from two guns mounted on her forecastle. The leader of the rebels was constantly in view, cheering on his men, and discharging his rifle as fast as he could reload. Frank fired several shots at him, and finding that, as usual, they were without effect, he asked the captain's permission to try a howitzer on him, which was granted. He ran below, trained the gun to his satisfaction, and waited for an opportunity to fire, during which the dispatch-boat came alongside and commenced putting off a supply of stores.

At length the rebel mounted the levee, and reigning in his horse, sat in his saddle gazing at the vessels, as if not at all concerned. He presented a fair mark, and Frank fired, but the shell went wild and burst in the woods, far beyond the rebel, who, however, beat a hasty retreat behind the levee.

"Oh, what a shot!" shouted a voice through the trumpet that led from the pilot-house to the main deck. "What a shot - altogether too much elevation."

"Who's that, I wonder?" soliloquized Frank. "It *was* a poor shot, but I'd like to see that fellow, whoever he is, do any better."

After giving orders to have the gun reloaded and secured, he ran into the wardroom to look after his mail, at the same time inquiring of every one he met, "Who was that making fun of my shooting?" But no one knew, nor cared to trouble himself about the matter, for the subject of conversation was, "We've got a new paymaster."

Frank was pleased to hear this, but was still determined to find the person who had laughed at his marksmanship, when he saw a pair of feet descending the ladder that led from the cabin to the pilot-house, and a moment afterward, a smart looking young officer, dressed in the uniform of a paymaster, stood in the wardroom, and upon discovering Frank, thrust out his hand and greeted him with -

"What a shot! Been in the service more than two years, and" -

"Why, Archie Winters, is this you?" exclaimed Frank, joyfully.

"*Paymaster* Winters, if you please" replied Archie, with mock dignity.

"How came you here? What are you doing? Got any money?" hurriedly inquired Frank.

"Got plenty of funds," replied his cousin. "But I say, Frank, how long has this fighting been going on?"

"Every day for the last week."

Archie shrugged his shoulders, and looked blank.

"I guess I had better go back to Cairo," said he; "these rebels, I hear, shoot very carelessly. Just before we came alongside here, I was standing on the deck of the dispatch-boat, and some fellow cracked away at me, sending the bullet altogether too close to my head for comfort."

"Oh, that's nothing, so long as he didn't hit you. You'll get used to that before you have been here a week. But, Archie, are you really ordered to this vessel?"

Archie at once produced his orders, and, sure enough, he was an acting assistant paymaster, and ordered to "report to the commanding officer of the U. S. S. Boxer for duty on board that vessel."

During the two years that Archie had been in the fleet-paymaster's office he had, by strict attention to his duties, worked his way up from "writer" to corresponding clerk. He had had ample opportunity to learn the duties of paymaster, and one day he suddenly took it into his head to make application for the position. He immediately wrote to his father, informing him of his intention, procured his letters of recommendation, and a month afterward received the appointment.

Hearing, through Frank, that the Boxer was without a paymaster, he succeeded in getting ordered to her, and, as he had not written to his cousin of his good fortune, the latter, as may be supposed, was taken completely by surprise.

Archie was speedily introduced to the officers of the vessel, who were pleased with his off-hand, easy manners, and delighted with the looks of a small safe which he had brought with him, for they knew, by the very particular orders he gave concerning it, that there was money in it.

At the end of an hour the rebels seemed to grow weary of the fight, for they drew off their forces; then, as soon as it was safe on deck, the cousins seated themselves on the guard, to "talk over old times." Frank gave descriptions of the fights in which he had engaged since they last met, and also related stories of mess-room life, with which Archie was entirely unacquainted; and to show him how things were conducted, told him of the jokes the officers frequently played upon each other.

"Speaking of jokes," said Archie, "reminds me of a little affair I had a hand in at Cairo.

"While the commandant of the station was absent on a leave, his place was supplied by a gentleman whom, for short, I will call Captain Smith. He was a regular officer, had grown gray in the service, and was one of the most eccentric men I ever saw. He was extremely nervous, too, and if a steamer happened to whistle while passing the wharf-boat, it would make him almost wild.

"One day, a man who lived off somewhere in the woods, came down to Cairo to get an appointment for his son as master's mate. Our office, you know, was just to the right of the door, and, if there was any thing that bothered me, it was for some body to stick his head over the railing when I was busy, and ask, 'Is the commandant of the station in?' There was an orderly on watch day and night, always ready to answer such questions, and besides, there was an abundance of notices on the walls pointing out the different offices; but in spite of this, every stranger that came in must stop and make inquiries of me.

"Well, this man came into the office, and as he had evidently never been there before, judging by the way he gaped at every thing, I told him that it was after office hours, and that he must call again the next morning about nine o'clock. He took a turn or two across the floor (by-the-way, he wore squeaking boots, that made a noise like a steam-whistle), and finally went out.

"The next evening, just as I was locking up my desk, he came in again, and I repeated what I had told him the night before, that he must come at nine o'clock in the *morning* - not at night - if he wished to see the captain, and he went out, after making noise enough with his squeaking boots to set a nervous man's teeth on edge. Now, would you believe it, that evening, after I had finished my work, and was starting out for supper, I saw this man coming up the stairs. He met me with the usual question, 'Is the captain in?' and I suddenly hit upon a plan to get rid of him, for I had made up my mind that the man didn't know what he was about; so I replied:

"'What do you want? Why don't you come here during our office hours, if you want to see me?'

"I spoke in a gruff voice, and I was so bundled up - for the night was very cold - that I knew he wouldn't recognize me.

"'I've been busy all day, cap'in,' said he; 'but the fact is' -

"I was afraid that I would be obliged to stand there in the cold and listen to a long, uninteresting yarn, so I interrupted him.

"'Speak quick, and don't keep me waiting.'

"'Wal, cap'in,' said he, 'I heerd you are in want of officers, an' I come to get a place for my son; I hear the wages are purty good.'

"'Yes,' I replied, 'we do want officers; but does your son know anything about a ship?'

"'Oh, yes? He's run the river as deck-hand for goin' nigh on to three year.'

"'Then he ought to know something, certainly. Come around tomorrow morning, at nine o'clock exactly, and I'll see what can be done for you. Now, mind, I say nine o'clock in the morning.'

"Well, the next morning, at the appointed time, to my utter astonishment, the man was on hand, and, as usual, commenced walking up and down the floor with his squeaking boots. The noise disturbed everyone within hearing, and presently the captain, who was in his office, and so busy that he hardly knew what he was about, spoke in a sharp tone:

"'Orderly, pull off those squeaking boots!'

"'It isn't me, sir.' said the orderly; 'it's a gentleman out here waiting to see you, sir.'

"'Then send him in - send him in at once, so that I can get rid of that noise.'

"The man was accordingly shown into the presence of the captain, while I listened with both ears to hear what was said.

"'Mornin', cap'in,' he began; 'I reckon I'm here on time.'

"'Time! what time? What do you want?' inquired the captain, who always spoke very fast, as though he were in a hurry to get through with what he had to say. 'What do you want, my good man. Be lively now.'

"'Why, cap'in, I come here to get that appointment for my son in this ere navy.'

"'Appointment! For your son!' repeated the captain. 'Who is he? I never heard of him.'

"'Wal, really now, cap'in, I'll be shot if you didn't tell me last night that you would make my son an officer. The wages are good, I hear, an' as I've a debt to pay off on the farm' -

"'Don't bother me!' interrupted the captain, beginning to get impatient.

"'But, cap'in,' urged the man, 'you can't bluff me off this 'ere way. You told me last night that you wanted officers; you know I met you on the stairs, and you promised, honor bright.'

"'Eh!' ejaculated the captain, in surprise,'my good man, allow me to know what I'm about, will you? *Will* you allow me to know myself? Orderly,' he continued, turning to that individual, who had stood by, convulsed with laughter, which he was vainly endeavoring to conceal, 'orderly, do you think this man is in his right mind?'

"The orderly said he didn't know; but, taking the man by the arm, showed him out of the office, telling him to come again, when the captain was not quite so busy.

"The conversation had been carried on in a loud tone, and all the occupants of the different offices had heard it, and were highly amused, for they knew that somebody had been playing a joke on the countryman; but it was a long time before I told anyone of the share I had had in the affair."

CHAPTER II

A NIGHT EXPEDITION

"The captain wishes to see you, gentlemen!" said the orderly, stepping up and saluting.

The cousins repaired to the cabin, and after Archie had been introduced to the captain (for being utterly ignorant of the manner in which things were conducted on shipboard, he had not yet reported his arrival), his orders were indorsed, and the captain, turning to his desk, ran his eye hastily over an official document, and said:

"Mr. Nelson, I have received instructions from the admiral to make you the executive officer of this vessel. Mr. Kearney's resignation has been accepted, and you will take his place. I am certain, from what I know and have heard of your past history, that I shall have no cause to regret the change."

After a few moments' conversation with the captain upon unimportant matters, the cousins returned to the wardroom.

Frank's constant attention to his duties had again been rewarded, and he was now the second in authority on board the vessel. All orders from the captain must pass through him, and in the absence of that gentleman he became commander. To say that Frank was delighted would but feebly express his feelings; he was proud of the honor, and determined that he would prove himself worthy of it. In fact, he had now reached the height of his ambition, although he had little dreamed that it would come so soon. He asked nothing more. He had worked hard and faithfully ever since he had entered the service, but in receiving the appointment of executive officer he felt amply rewarded.

He was young in years for so responsible a position, but he had no fears of his ability to perform all the duties required of him, for the routine of ship life had become as familiar to him as was the road from Lawrence to his quiet little home on the banks of Glen's Creek. But his promotion did not affect him as it does a great many who suddenly find themselves possessed of power. He did not "stand upon his rank," nor in his intercourse with his messmates endeavor to keep constantly before their minds the fact that he was the second in command. Those who have been in the service - especially in the navy - will recall to mind incidents of this character; but our hero never forgot the respect he owed to his superiors, and his conduct toward those under him was marked by the same kindness he had always shown them.

Frank knew that he had something of a task before him. Although he could now turn into his bunk at night without being called upon to stand his regular watch, he had more difficult duties to perform. He was responsible for the manner in which affairs were conducted about decks, for the neat appearance of the vessel and of the men; and as the former executive officer had been rather careless in this respect, Frank knew that his first move must be made in that direction.

For the next two days, as the rebels did not trouble them, Frank worked early and late, and the results of his labor were soon made apparent. Every one remarked the improved appearance of the men, who, at the Sunday morning muster, appeared on deck in spotless uniforms and well-blacked shoes. After the roll had been called, and the captain, in company with Frank, proceeded to inspect the vessel, the young officer knew that his improvements had been appreciated when the former, who was an old sailor, said, with a smile of satisfaction:

Harry Castlemon

"Mr. Nelson, this begins to look something like a ship, sir. This really looks like business. The admiral may come here now and inspect the vessel as soon as he pleases."

The next morning, as Frank sat at the table in the wardroom, engaged in answering the letters he had received by the dispatch-boat, and Archie was in his office straightening out his books and papers, a bullet came suddenly crashing through the cabin - a signal that the rebels had again made their appearance. Frank, who had become accustomed to such interruptions, deliberately wiped his pen, corked his ink-stand, and was carefully putting away his letters, when there was a hurrying of feet in the office; the door flew open, and Archie, divested of his coat, bounded into the cabin, exclaiming:

"A fellow can't tell when he's safe in this country. I wish I was back in the fleet-paymaster's office. I wouldn't mind a good fair fight, but this thing of being shot at when you least expect it isn't pleasant."

As Archie spoke, he hurriedly seized a gun from the rack, which had been put up in the cabin in order to have weapons close at hand, and sprang up the ladder that led into the pilothouse. Frank, although he laughed heartily at his cousin's rapid movements, was a good deal surprised, for he had always believed him to be possessed of a good share of courage. It would, however, have tried stronger nerves than Archie's; but men who had become familiar with such scenes, who had learned to regard them merely as something disagreeable which could not be avoided, could not sympathize with one in his situation, and many a wink was exchanged, and many a laugh indulged in, at the expense of the "green paymaster."

When Frank had put away his writing materials, he ran below to see that the ports were all closed; after which he returned to the wardroom, and, securing a rifle, went into the pilot-house, where he found Archie engaged in reloading his gun, while the officers were complimenting him on a fine shot he had just made.

"Mr. Nelson," exclaimed the doctor, as Frank made his appearance, "I guess your white horseman is done for now. The paymaster lifted him out of his saddle as clean as a whistle."

Frank looked out at one of the ports, and, sure enough, there was the white horse running riderless about, and his wounded master was being carried behind the levee. The officers continued to fire as often as a rebel showed himself, but the latter seemed to have lost all desire for fighting, for they retreated to the plantation-house which stood back from the river, out of range of the rifles, where they gathered in a body as if in consultation, now and then setting up defiant yells, which came faintly to the ears of those in the pilot-house.

"They are saucy enough now that they are out of harm's way," said Archie, turning to his cousin. But the latter made no reply. He stood leaning on his rifle, gazing at the guerrillas, as if busily engaged with his own thoughts, and finally left the pilot-house and sought an interview with the captain.

"I have been thinking, sir," said he, as he entered the cabin and took the chair offered him, "that if that house out there had been burned long ago, we should not have had ten men killed by those guerrillas. They seem to use that building as their head-quarters, and if it could be destroyed they would cease to trouble us."

"That's my opinion," replied the captain. "But who is to undertake the job? Who's to go out there, in the face of three or four hundred rebels, and do it? *I* can't, with a crew of only fifty men."

"I didn't suppose it could be done openly, sir; but couldn't it be accomplished by stratagem in the night, for instance?"

The captain shook his head; but Frank, who was not yet discouraged, continued:

"I have not made this proposition, captain, without thinking it all over - without taking into consideration all the chances for and against it - and I still think it could be accomplished."

"Well, how would you go to work?" asked the captain, settling back in his chair with the air of a man who had made his decision, from which he was not to be turned.

Frank then proceeded to recount the plans he had laid for the accomplishment of his object, to which the captain listened attentively, and when Frank had ceased, he rose to his feet and paced the cabin. He knew that the young officer had before engaged in expeditions similar to the one he now proposed, when, in carrying out his designs, he had exhibited the skill and judgment of a veteran. In the present instance, his plans were so well laid, that there appeared to be but little chance for failure. After a few moments' consideration, the captain again seated himself, and said:

"Well, Mr. Nelson, it shall be as you propose. If you succeed, I am certain that this guerrilla station will be broken up; if you fail, it will only be what many a good officer has done before you."

"I assure you, sir, I shall leave no plan untried to insure my success," replied Frank, as he left the cabin.

"What's the matter now?" inquired Archie, as his cousin entered the wardroom. "Been getting a blowing up already?"

"Oh, no!" replied Frank. "Come in here, and I'll tell you all about it;" and he drew Archie into the office, where he proceeded to tell him all that had been determined upon. When he had finished, the latter exclaimed:

"I want to go with you. Will you take me?"

Frank thought of Archie's behavior but a few moments before, and wondered what use he could posssibly be in an expedition like the one proposed.

"If you do go," he answered, at length, "you'll be sorry for it. It requires those who are accustomed to such business; and you have never been in an action in your life. The undertaking is dangerous."

"I don't care if it is," answered Archie. "That's just the reason why I want to go - to be with you; and I warrant you I'll stick to you as long as any body."

"Besides," began Frank, "if any thing should happen to you" -

"I'm just as likely to get back as you are," replied Archie, excitedly, "and I want to go."

After considerable urging, Frank finally asked and obtained permission for Archie to accompany the expedition, at which the latter was overjoyed. He was very far from realizing the danger there was in the undertaking, and had as little idea of what would be required of him as he had of the moon.

The cousins passed the afternoon in the pilothouse, watching the movements of the guerrillas through spy-glasses, studying the "lay of the land," the directions in which the different roads ran - in short, nothing was omitted which they thought might be useful for them to know. Just before night a storm set in; the wind blew, and the rain fell in torrents; and, although Frank regarded it as something in their favor, under any other circumstances he would have preferred tumbling into bed to venturing out in it. The hammocks were not piped as usual, but all hands were to remain on deck during the night, to be ready to lend assistance in case it was required. At ten o'clock the cutter lay alongside the vessel, the crew were in their places, and Frank and his cousin, surrounded by the officers who had assembled to see them off, stood on the guards ready to start.

"Paymaster," said Frank, turning to his cousin, "hadn't you better remain on board?" (He addressed him as paymaster, for, of course, it would have been contrary to naval rules to call him by his given name in the presence of the captain.)

"No, sir," answered Archie, quickly buttoning up his pea-jacket with a resolute air. "Do you suppose I'm going to back out now? If you do, you are mistaken. I'm not afraid of a little rain."

Frank made no reply, but, after shaking hands with the captain and officers, followed his cousin into the cutter, which floated off into the darkness amid the whispered wishes for "good luck" from all the ship's company who had witnessed its departure. Frank took the helm, and turned the boat down the river. Not an oar was used, for the young officer did not know but the rebels had posted sentries along the bank, whom the least splashing in the water would alarm. Archie sat beside his cousin, with his collar pulled up over his ears, and his hands thrust into the pockets of his pea-jacket, heartily wishing that Frank had chosen a pleasanter night for their expedition. For half an hour they floated along with the current in silence, until Frank, satisfied that he had gone far enough down the river to get below the sentries, if any were posted on the bank, gave the order to use the oars, and turned the cutter's head toward the shore, which they reached in a few moments.

The crew quietly disembarked, and as the sailors gathered about him, Frank said,

"Now, men, I'm going to leave you here until the paymaster and myself can go up to the house, and accomplish what we have come for. Tom," he added, turning to the coxswain of the cutter, "you will have charge of the boat, and remember you are in no case to leave her. We may be discovered, and get into a fight. If we do, and are cut off from the river and unable to get back, I'll whistle, and you will at once answer me, so that I may know that you hear me, and pull off to the vessel. We'll take care of ourselves. Do you understand?"

The crew of the cutter were old sailors - men who had

followed the sea through storm and sunshine all their lives. They had been in more than one action, too, during the rebellion, and had gladly volunteered for the expedition, supposing that they were to accompany Frank wherever he went. During the short time the latter had been on board the Boxer, they had become very much attached to him. Although he was a very strict officer, and always expected every man to do his duty promptly, he always treated them with the greatest kindness, and never spoke harshly to them. This was so different from the treatment they had usually received at the hands of their officers, that it won their hearts; and, although they admired his courage, they would have felt much better pleased had they received orders to accompany him.

"Don't you understand, Tom?" again asked Frank, seeing that the coxswain hesitated.

"Oh, yes, sir," replied the sailor, touching his hat; "I understand, sir. But, Mr. Nelson, may I be so bold as to ask one question - one favor, I may say?"

"Certainly; speak it out," answered Frank, who little imagined what thoughts were passing through the minds of his men. "What is it? Do you wish to go back to the ship, and leave us here alone?"

"No, sir," answered all the men in a breath.

"Mr. Nelson," said the coxswain, "I never yet refused duty because there was danger in it, and I'm too old a man to begin now. You have here, sir, twelve as good men as ever trod a ship's deck, and you know, sir, that when you passed the word for volunteers for this expedition, you didn't have to call twice. But we all thought that we should go with you to the end; and, to tell the truth, sir, we don't like the idea of you and the paymaster going off alone among them rebels. You are sure to get into trouble, and we want to go with you."

On more than one occasion had Frank been made aware of the

affection his men cherished for him, and he felt as proud of it as he did of the uniform he wore; but he had never been more affected than he was on the present occasion.

"Men," he answered, in a voice that was none of the steadiest, "I assure you I appreciate the interest you take in my welfare, and were I going to fight, I should certainly take you with me; but sometimes two can accomplish more than a dozen. Besides, I promised the captain that I would leave you here, and I must do so. Now, remember and pull off to the vessel if you hear me whistle."

"Yes, sir," replied the coxswain; "but it'll be the first time I ever deserted an officer in trouble."

The sailors were evidently far from being pleased with this arrangement, but they were allowed no opportunity to oppose it, even had they felt inclined to do so, for Frank and his cousin speedily disappeared in the darkness.

CHAPTER III

ARCHIE IN A PREDICAMENT

As soon as the young officers had reached the top of the bank, they paused to take their bearings, and to select some landmark that would enable them to easily find the boat again. Away off in the darkness they saw the twinkling of a light, which they knew was in the house which the guerrillas were using as their head-quarters.

"Now, Archie," said Frank, "take a good look at this big tree here" (pointing to the object in question) "so that you will know it again. The boat lies in the river exactly in a line with that tree. Now, if you should be separated from me and discovered, make straight for the cutter. But if you are cut off from it, run up the river until you get a little above where the vessel lies, and then jump in and swim out to her. Do you understand?"

"Yes," replied Archie.

"Be careful of your weapons," continued his cousin, "and keep them dry and ready for instant use. Don't be captured - whatever you do, don't be captured!"

"I'll look out for that," answered Archie "But, Frank," he continued, "why did you tell the men to pull back to the vessel if we should be cut off from the river? I should think that would be just the time you would want them to remain."

"Why," replied Frank, "the very first thing the rebels would think of, if we were discovered, would be to capture our boat, and while part of them were after us, the others would run to the river and gobble up boat, crew, and all. Then they would know that we were still on shore, and would scour the country to find us. But if the boat goes off to the vessel, the rebels will be more than half inclined to believe that we have gone off too, and, consequently, will not take the pains to hunt us which they would do if they *knew* we were still on shore. But let us be moving; we've no time to waste."

Frank started toward the house, carefully picking his way over the wet, slippery ground, now and then pausing to listen, and to reconnoiter as well as the darkness would permit, and finally stopped scarcely a stone's throw from the building. Not a guerrilla had they seen. Not dreaming that the "yankee gunboatmen" would have the audacity to attack them when they knew the rebels were so far superior in numbers, the latter had neglected to post sentries, and Frank was satisfied that their approach had not been discovered.

"Now, Archie," said he, as they drew up behind a tree for concealment, "you stay here, and I'll see if I can set fire to that house."

"There are people in it," said his cousin; "I just saw a man pass by that window where the light is."

"Then they must look out for themselves," answered Frank. "That's what we have to do when they shoot into our cabin. Now, you stay here, and if you hear any shooting, run for the boat."

"What will *you* do?" asked Archie.

"Oh, I'll take care of myself. Good-bye."

As Frank spoke he moved silently toward the house, and was soon out of sight.

"Now," soliloquized Archie, "I am to stay here, am I? That's what I was ordered to do, but I don't know whether I'll obey or not. It is evident Frank left me here to keep me out of harm's way. Perhaps he thinks that because I have never smelt powder, I am a coward; but I'll show him that I am not."

So saying, Archie stepped out from behind his tree, and walked slowly toward the house. When he arrived opposite the window from which the light shone, he stopped and looked in. He did not, however, go up close to the window, or he certainly would have been seen; but he remained standing at a respectful distance, so that he would have some chance for escape, in case he should be discovered.

The sight that met his gaze would have been sufficient to deter most men from attempting to burn the house. The room was filled with men, some of whom were lying on the floor on their blankets, others sitting around the table, and one or two were walking about the apartment. In the corner stood their arms, ready to be seized at a moment's warning. And this was but one of the rooms; perhaps the whole house was filled with guerrillas.

"My eye!" said Archie to himself, "what a hornet's nest would be raised about our ears, if we should be discovered."

His heart beat faster than usual, as he moved back from the window, and walked silently around to the other side of the house. Here also was a window, from which a light shone, and as, like the other, it was destitute of a curtain, every thing that went on within could be plainly seen by Archie, who took his station behind some bushes that stood at a little distance from the house. The room had three occupants, whom Archie at once set down as officers. One of them carried his arm in a sling. He was a tall, powerful-looking man, and Archie recognized in him the daring rider of the white horse - the chief of the guerrillas.

"I wonder what the old chap would say if he knew I was

about," thought Archie - "I, who gave him that wound. I'd be booked for Shreveport, certain."

He was interrupted in his meditations by the movements of the officers, who arose and approached the door, bringing their chairs with them. The storm had ceased, and as there was no longer any necessity of remaining in the house, the rebels were, no doubt, moving to cooler quarters. Archie at once thought of retreating; but the thought had scarcely passed through his mind, when the door opened, the rebels walked out on the portico, and seating themselves in their chairs, deposited their feet on the railing; while the young officer stretched himself out behind the bush, heartily wishing that he could sink into the ground out of sight.

"A very warm evening, colonel," said one of the rebels, fanning himself with his hat.

"Very," answered the guerrilla chief, gently moving his wounded arm, little dreaming that the one who gave him that wound was at that very moment lying behind the bushes into which he had just thrown the stump of his cigar. "It's very warm. I wish I had that rascally Yank that shot me," he added, "this wound is very painful."

Archie upon hearing this was almost afraid that the beating of his heart, which thumped against his ribs with a noise that frightened him, would certainly reveal to the rebels the fact that the "rascally Yank" was then in their immediate vicinity.

"But, if our plans work," continued the colonel, "in less than a week from this time they will all be on the way to Shreveport."

"May I ask, colonel," said the one who had not yet spoken, "how soon those boats will be ready?"

"Major Jackson reports that they will be finished by to-morrow night, and it will take all of one day to run them down the creek to the river."

"Then by Thursday evening," said the one who had first spoken, "we may be ready to make the attempt."

"Yes, if the night is favorable."

"But, colonel, all these gun-boats are supplied with hot water, and that, you know, is the worst kind of an enemy to fight. Men will run from that who wouldn't flinch before cold steel."

"Oh, we must take the Yanks by surprise, of course. The boats will hold fifty men each, and we must drop down the river so that we will land one on each side of the vessel. If the night is dark - and we shall not make the attempt unless it is - we can get within pistol-shot of her before we are discovered, and by the time their men get fairly out of bed she's ours. Hark! what noise was that?"

The rebels listened for a moment, and one of them replied:

"I didn't hear any thing."

"Well, *I* did," returned the colonel, "and it sounded very much like some one shouting for help. I'm certain I heard it."

Archie, who lay in his concealment, trembling like a leaf, was also confident that *he* had heard something that sounded like a call for assistance. What if it was Frank in danger, and shouting to the cutter's crew for help? The thought to Archie was a terrible one, and he forgot the dangers of his own situation, and thought only of his cousin. But if Frank was in trouble, why did he not give the signal to the cutter's crew? Archie waited and listened for it, but did not hear it given.

While these thoughts were passing through his mind, the rebels sat on the portico listening, and at length the colonel said:

"I know I hear something now, but it is the tramping of a horse. I suppose it is Tibbs, coming with the mail."

The colonel's surmise proved to be correct, for in a few moments a man rode up, and dismounting so close to Archie that the latter could have touched him, tied his horse to the very bush which formed his concealment; then, throwing a pair of well-filled saddle-bags across his shoulder, he ran up the steps, saying:

"Good evening, gentlemen. What! colonel, are you wounded?" he added, on seeing the rebel's bandaged arm.

"Yes; this makes four times I have been shot while in the service. But how is the mail?"

"Rather heavy," answered the man. "If you have any letters to go, you will have to furnish another bag - these are full."

"All right," said the colonel; then raising his voice, he called out, "Bob! Bob! Where is that black rascal?"

"Heyar, sar," answered a voice, and presently a negro came around the corner of the house, and removing his tattered hat, stood waiting for orders.

"Bob," said the colonel, "tell Stiles that the mail is all ready to go across the river."

Stiles! How Frank would have started could he have heard that name! He would have known then, had he not before been aware of the fact, that he was again among *Colonel Harrison's Louisiana Wild-cats.*

The negro, in obedience to his orders, disappeared, but soon returned, with the intelligence that Stiles was not to be found.

"Not to be found," echoed the colonel; "that's twice he has failed me. But this mail must not be delayed. Tell Damon I want to see him."

The negro again disappeared, and in a few moments came

back with a soldier, to whom the colonel said:

"Damon, here's a mail that must go across the river to-night. Can you pull an oar?"

"Yas," replied the man.

"Then get some one to go with you, and start at once. The skiff, you know, is in the creek, just above where that Yankee gun-boat lies."

"Yas," answered the man again, as he took the mail-bags which the colonel handed him.

"This one," continued the rebel, pointing to a small canvas bag which one of his officers had just brought out of the house - "this one contains my mail - all official documents, to go to Richmond. Be careful of it. Don't let the Yankees get hold of you."

"No," replied the soldier, as he shouldered the mail and disappeared.

The conversation that followed, of which Archie heard every word, served to convince him that, although the rebels kept up a bold front, and appeared sanguine of success in their attempts to destroy the Government, yet among themselves they acknowledged their c ause to beutterly hopeless unless some bold stroke could be made to "dishearten the Yankees."

In spite of Archie's dangerous situation, which had tried his nerves severely, he listened to every word that was uttered, and even became interested in what the rebels were saying. Now and then he was called to a sense of his situation by the movements of the horse, which, being restive, came very near stepping on him as he pranced about.

Damon had been gone about half an hour, and the colonel had just commenced explaining to the man who had brought the mail the manner in which the capture of the Boxer was to be effected, when suddenly the report of a pistol startled every one on the portico. A moment afterward came another, which was followed by a yell of agony.

"What's that?" exclaimed the colonel, springing from his chair in alarm. "Are we attacked? Get out there, every mother's son of you!" he continued, as the men, having been aroused by the noise, came pouring out of the rooms in which they were quartered. "Every man able to draw a saber get out there! Run for the river! That's where the reports sounded, and if there are any boats there capture them. That will keep the Yankees on shore, and we can hunt them up at our leisure!"

The men ran out of the house and started for the river at the top of their speed, at the same time yelling with all the strength of their lungs, while the colonel and his officers ran into their room, and hastily seizing such weapons as came first to their hands, followed after. To describe Archie's feelings, as he lay there behind that bush and listened to the sounds of pursuit, were impossible. The noise the rebels made seemed to bewilder him completely, for he lay on the ground several moments, it seemed to him, without the power to move hand or foot.

Suddenly the thought struck him that now was the time to accomplish the object of the expedition. The house was deserted, and the yells, which grew fainter and fainter, told him that the rebels were getting further away. Yes, it was now or never. In an instant, Archie's courage and power of action returned. Springing to his feet, he ran to the end of the portico, on which were piled several bales of hay and bundles of fodder, which the rebels no doubt intended for their horses. But Archie determined that they should be put to a different use, for he quickly drew from his pocket two large bottles filled with coal oil, which he threw over the hay. He then applied a match, and in an instant it was in a blaze. He waited a moment to see it fairly started, and then sprang off the portico. As he passed the door, he heard an ejaculation of surprise, followed by the report of a pistol, and the noise of a bullet as it whizzed past his head. It frightened him, and at the same time acted upon him as the crack of a whip does upon a spirited horse; for when the rebel who fired the shot had reached the portico, Archie had disappeared in the darkness.

CHAPTER IV

A MARK FOR THE UNION

Let us now return to Frank, whom we left setting out for the house, after having given Archie emphatic instructions to remain behind the tree until his return. He did not feel at all at his ease after he had left his cousin, for he might have stationed him in the most dangerous place that could have been found; and what if Archie should be discovered and captured? He was well enough acquainted with his cousin's disposition to know that he would not surrender without a fight; but what could he do when opposed by a regiment of veteran rebels? Frank thought not of his own peril, for that was something he had fully expected to encounter before he started. This was not the first time he had voluntarily placed himself in danger; but with Archie the case was different; and Frank was several times on the point of returning to his cousin and making use of his authority, as commander of the expedition, to send him back to the boat. By the time these thoughts had passed through his mind, he had reached a log-cabin which stood at a little distance from the house; and as he halted behind it, to shelter himself from the storm, still debating upon the course he ought to pursue in regard to Archie, some one inside the cabin commenced singing - "I'll lay ten dollars down And chuck 'em up one by one!"

If there was any more of the song, the rebel evidently did not know it, for he kept singing these two lines over and over, now and then varying the monotony of the performance by whistling. Frank stood for some moments listening to him, and finally began moving cautiously around the cabin, to find some opening through which he could look and see what was going on inside. He presently discovered a hole between the logs, and, upon looking in, saw a man seated on the floor before a fire-place, in which burned some pine knots, engaged in whittling out an oar with his bowie-knife. On the floor near him lay one evidently just finished. At the opposite side of the room stood a bag, from the mouth of which peeped several letters.

A thought struck Frank - which would be of the most benefit, to burn the house or to capture the mail, which might contain information of the greatest importance? Undoubtedly the latter would be of the most consequence. Then he debated long and earnestly upon the chances of escaping with the mail, should he attempt its capture. The man who had charge of it was a most powerful-looking fellow, who knowing the importance of his trust, and the certainty of receiving prompt and effective assistance from his comrades, would, no doubt, fight most desperately, unless he could be taken at disadvantage and secured before he had time to think of resistance. Besides, the cabin was scarcely fifty feet distant from the house, which Frank knew was filled with men, for he could hear them walking about the rooms and talking to each other. The least unusual noise would certainly alarm them, in which case escape would be entirely out of the question Frank, we say, thought over all these things, and finally coming to the conclusion that it would be worse than useless to attempt the capture of the mail, turned his attention to the house. How was he to set fire to it?

Frank, we know, was not wanting in courage, but he had learned, by experience, that there are times when "discretion is the better part of valor." When he proposed the expedition, he had not expected to find the entire regiment quartered in the house. He had supposed that the men would find sleeping-rooms in the negro quarters, which were nearly a half mile back, while the house would be reserved for the officers. But the rebels surely would not remain up all night, and when they had all gone to bed would be the time to execute his purpose. He would not abandon his project until he had given it a trial, or fully satisfied himself that the undertaking was utterly impracticable. For the present, he would remain where he was; something might "turn up" which would be to his advantage.

At this moment a man entered the cabin, the door of which stood open, and inquired:

"Going over to-night, Stiles?"

Frank was thunderstruck, and he now saw the necessity of attempting nothing unless it promised complete success. As the reader has already learned, he was among his old enemies, the Wildcats. Upon making this discovery he was both astonished and alarmed - astonished, for it seemed to him that he could scarcely make a move in any direction without being confronted by the redoubtable Wild-cats. This was the second time he had found himself among them before he was aware of it. He was alarmed, because he knew, by experience, the treatment he would receive if he should fall into their hands without the prospect of an immediate exchange.

But his attention was again drawn to the men in the cabin.

"Yes," replied Stiles, in answer to his companion's question, "I'm going over to-night - allers makin' due 'lowance for bein' ketched by the Yanks."

"Here's some mail, then," continued the man, thrusting several letters into the bag. "How soon do you start?"

"Jest as soon as Tibbs comes with the up-country mail, an' I get the kernel's letters. Was you takin' a chaw of tobaker, Bob?"

"No, I wasn't," replied the other, quickly thrusting his hand into his pocket, as if to protect the precious article. "Tobacco is scarce."

"Now, Bob," said Stiles, "I know you've got some. Me an' you's allers been good friends."

The rebel could not withstand this appeal, although he produced his "plug" very reluctantly, and as he handed it to his companion, said:

"Stiles, you're a dead beat. Go easy on that, now, if you please, because it's all there is in the regiment."

The rebel cut off a huge piece of the weed, and, thrusting it into his cheek, went on with his work, while Bob returned to his quarters. He had scarcely quitted the cabin before Frank had all his plans laid. He would go back after Archie, and together they would lie in wait on the bank of the river, and, if possible, capture that mail. With this determination, he was moving slowly away from the cabin, when a door, which he had not before noticed, suddenly opened, and Stiles came out, and turning the corner, stood face to face with Frank, and scarcely an arm's length from him. With the latter, retreat without discovery was, of course, impossible. There was but one course he could pursue, and that presented but a small chance for success. He was, however, allowed no time for deliberation, for the rebel, quickly recovering from his surprise, turned to run; but with one bound Frank overtook him, and throwing him to the ground, caught him by the throat, stifling a cry for help that arose to his lips. This it was that had alarmed the colonel and Archie; and had the former investigated the matter, Frank would again have been a prisoner in the hands of the Wild-cats.

Stiles struggled desperately to free himself from the strong grasp that held him, until Frank pulled one of his revolvers from the pocket of his pea-jacket and presented it at his head.

"Do you surrender?" he asked, releasing his hold of the rebel's throat.

"Yes," replied Stiles, faintly. "Don't shoot, Yank!"

"You shall not be harmed if you behave yourself. Have you any weapons?"

"No! They are all in the shanty!"

Frank, after searching the rebel's pockets and satisfying himself of the truth of this statement, continued:

"Get up! Now, I know you have friends all around you, but if you have the least desire to live, you'll not make any noise; although you may alarm the camp, it will not save you. Do you understand?"

"Have I got a pair of ears?" asked the rebel.

"Well, if you have, you hear what I say," returned Frank. "Now go this way," he added, pointing toward the river.

The rebel, who had a wholesome fear of the revolver which Frank held in his hand, ready cocked, obeyed, without the slightest hesitation, and they reached the bank of the river, where the cutter lay, without being discovered.

"Now," said Frank, "I want to ask you a few questions. Where do you keep the boat in which you were going to carry that mail?"

"In the creek, jest above where that ar' gunboat lies, replied Stiles."

"How many of you were to go?"

"Two - me an' another feller."

"Well, now, the colonel won't find you when he wants you. What will he do?"

"Oh, he'll send some body else. The mail must go, an' it makes no odds who takes it, so long as he don't get ketched."

"That's all I want to know," said Frank. Then, going to the top of the bank, he called out:

"Tom, come up here!"

The coxswain soon made his appearance, and Frank said:

"Now, Stiles, you're a prisoner."

"Dog gone ef I keer," he replied, "so long as I get plenty of grub an' tobaker."

The rebel was marched down the bank, and Frank again bent his steps toward the house, intending to find his cousin, and, with his assistance, to capture the mail. When he arrived at the tree where he had left Archie, the latter was not to be seen. This, however, did not give him any uneasiness, for Archie, he thought, had doubtless gone back to the cutter. Frank had already made up his mind to go back after him, when he saw a man walk up to the cabin in which he had first discovered the man who was now his prisoner, and heard him call out:

"Massa Stiles! de mail all ready, sar!"

Receiving no answer, the negro walked into the cabin, but finding it vacant, went out to make the report to the colonel that Stiles was not to be found. From this Frank knew that he had no time to lose. Stiles had told him that some one else would be sent with the mail, and as it was all ready, a man would soon be found to take his place. If he went back after Archie, he might be too late. He must attempt it alone, and unaided. Walking out from behind the tree, he started toward the creek, where lay the boat in which the mail was to be carried.

The creek he found without difficulty; but the boat was

evidently hidden away, for he searched up and down the bank for it without success. If he found it, it was his intention to cut it loose, and allow it to drift out into the river, thus depriving the rebels of the means of carrying their mail. But failing in this, he ran up the bank, and awaited the coming of the rebels. It was a hazardous undertaking to attempt the capture of two men, both of whom were, no doubt, well armed; but Frank had great confidence in the *looks* of his revolvers, and hoped to accomplish his object without alarming the rebels in the house.

He had waited perhaps a quarter of an hour, when he heard footsteps approaching, and presently he discovered the two men for whom he had been watching. One carried the mail-bags, and the other a pair of oars, the same, no doubt, which Stiles had but a short time before completed. Frank waited until they were almost upon him, and then sprang up with a revolver in each hand, which he pointed straight at the heads of the men, exclaiming:

"You're my prisoners. Don't make any resistance."

The rebels were astonished, and the man who carried the mail-bags threw them down and held his arms above his head, in token of surrender. But the other, after regarding the officer for a moment, as if to make sure that it was a human being with whom he had to deal, dropped his oars, and before his captor was aware of his intention, drew a pistol and fired. Frank felt a sharp pain in his left shoulder, and the revolver which he held in that hand fell from his grasp. He had received his first wound, but although thoroughly frightened, he did not lose his presence of mind. If he had, he would soon have been recalled to a sense of his dangerous situation, for the rebel again cocked his revolver; but this time Frank fired first, and the rebel sank to the ground with a loud yell. In an instant Frank turned upon the other; but he appeared to be too much under the influence of fear to lend his comrade any assistance.

All thought of concealment was now out of the question. The

rebels in the house had, of course, been alarmed, and Frank's only chance for escape with his prisoner and the mail was to reach the cutter as soon as possible, and pull off to the vessel. Hastily relieving the prisoner of his weapons, he directed him to pick up the mail and follow the course he pointed out.

The prisoner did as he was ordered; but they had not gone far when a loud yelling announced that the rebels in the house had been alarmed, and were in pursuit. Frank kept close behind his prisoner, who, through fear of the revolver, ran at a rapid rate, but they had further to run to reach the cutter than the guerrillas, and the latter gained rapidly. The prisoner, who was not long in discovering this, slackened his pace considerably, although he appeared to be doing his utmost. Frank, however, was not deceived. Thrusting his revolver into his pocket, he seized the rebel by the nape of the neck, and helped him over the ground in a manner more rapid than agreeable. Had the man been aware of the fact that his captor had but one arm that he could use, he might not have submitted so quietly as he did. Frank, whose whole mind was wrapped up in the idea of saving his prisoner and the mail, did not stop to think of this, but pushed his man ahead to such good advantage that they succeeded in reaching the cutter before their pursuers. He marched the rebel down the bank in the most lively manner, and tumbled him into the boat, where he was instantly seized and secured.

The sailors, who had heard the noise of the pursuit, and waited impatiently for the appearance of their officer, were all in their places, and as Frank sprang in, he shouted:

"Shove off - lively now, lads!"

The cutter was speedily pushed from the shore, and the oars got out and handled by twelve strong fellows, all good oarsmen.

"Let fall - give away together," again commanded Frank, who, in spite of the pain of his wound, began to chuckle over his good luck in securing the mail. "The rebs will give us a volley," he continued, "unless we get out of sight in the darkness before they reach the bank. So, pick her up, lads, and walk right away with her."

The sailors, understanding the order, and rejoicing in the escape of their young officer, whose safety and well-being they regarded as infinitely of more importance than their own, gave way manfully on the muffled oars, which made no sound as they bent beneath the sturdy strokes, and the cutter flew noiselessly through the water, The rebels reached the bank but a few moments after the cutter had left, but neither seeing nor hearing any thing of her, they contented themselves with uttering their yells, and firing a volley into the darkness in the direction they supposed the boat had gone.

But their attention was soon called to another quarter, for a bright flame shot up from the house. The boat's crew saw it, and could scarcely refrain hurrahing; but knowing that they were not yet out of range of the guerrillas' rifles, they gave vent to their jubilant feelings by redoubling their efforts at the oars.

"Mr. Nelson," whispered the coxswain, "may I be allowed to say that was well done, sir!"

"I didn't do that, Tom," answered Frank, in a faint voice, as he gazed in surprise at the burning house, and thought of his cousin. "Is Paymaster Winters in the cutter?"

Frank hardly dared to ask the question, for if his cousin had been in the boat he would have known it before that time.

"The paymaster!" repeated the coxswain; "no, sir. He went away with you, sir, and I haven't seen him since. He's missing, that's a fact."

Frank felt ready to faint on hearing this, and very bitterly did he censure himself for allowing his cousin to accompany him! But regrets were useless; the mischief had been done, and could not be undone. He had one hope, however, to which he still clung - that Archie might be on board the vessel. Perhaps, not daring to attempt to find his way back to the cutter, through fear of capture, he had swam on board and was now safe. He would soon know.

In a few moments they had reached the Boxer, and as the cutter came along side, Frank seized the mail-bags and sprang out. After giving the officer of the deck, who met him at the gangway, instructions in regard to the prisoners, he ran up the stairs that led to the wardroom. Here he met the captain, who, taking him familiarly by the arm, led him into the cabin, exclaiming:

"Mr. Nelson, I congratulate you, sir; it was well done, sir! The house is all in a blaze."

"Captain," said Frank, "I didn't do that, sir. Is the paymaster on board?

"Why, no, sir; not unless he came with you."

"I haven't seen him, captain, since I left him within a short distance of that house. If he is not on board, sir, he's out there yet, and he has fired the building."

"Why, Mr. Nelson," exclaimed the captain, for the first time noticing Frank's pale face and useless hand, from which the blood was dripping, "you are wounded, sir. Orderly, orderly, send the doctor here at once."

CHAPTER V

A RUN FOR LIFE

Archie was as light of foot as an antelope, and fear lent him wings. In obedience to his cousin's instructions, he ran up the river, directing his course through a thick woods, jumping over logs and making his way through the bushes with a rapidity that surprised himself. The rebel who had discovered him followed for a short distance, but finding that he was losing ground, he stopped and fired his revolver in the direction he supposed Archie had gone; but the bullets went wide of the mark, and the latter, who now regarded his escape as a thing beyond a doubt, laughed when he thought how cleverly he had accomplished the object of the expedition.

Having reached a safe distance from the house, he stopped and listened. He distinctly heard the crackling of flames, and presently a bright light shone over the trees. The building was fairly in a blaze. He was, however, allowed scarcely a moment to congratulate himself, for the yells of the guerrillas plainly told him that they had discovered the fire, and were commencing pursuit. Archie again set out, intent on reaching clear ground as soon as possible, for he knew that no plan would be left untried to capture him. His situation was still any thing but a pleasant one, but he was sanguine of reaching the vessel in safety, until a long-drawn-out bay came echoing through the woods, and drove the blood back upon his heart. The rebels were following him with a blood-hound!

For a moment Archie staggered as though he had been struck a severe blow by some unseen hand, but quickly realizing the fact that his safety depended upon his own exertions and the use he made of the next few moments, he speedily recovered his presence of mind, and hastily securing his revolvers, which, up to this time, he had carried in the pockets of his pea-jacket, he pulled off that garment, and throwing it on the ground, started off at the top of his speed.

Being thus relieved of a great incumbrance, he made headway rapidly, but, fast as he ran, he heard that dreadful sound coming nearer, mingled with loud yells of triumph from the pursuing rebels He had, with surprise and indignation, listened to Frank's description of his run from Shreveport, when he and his companions had been pursued with blood-hounds, little imagining that he would ever be placed in a similar situation.

And how did it happen that he had not aroused the hound while he was about the house? Had he moved so silently that the animal had not heard him, or had he been in the building with the men? This question Archie could not answer. But one thing was certain, and that was that the hound was, at that very moment, on his trail, and unless he soon reached the river his capture was beyond a doubt. He, however, had no fears of being overpowered by the hound. He fully realized the fact that he would soon be overtaken, and had resolved to shoot the animal the moment he made his appearance.

The yells of the rebels grew fainter, and Archie knew he was gaining on them. This gave him encouragement. In fact, since the hound had opened on his trail, after the first momentary feeling of terror had vanished, he had retained his coolness in a remarkable degree, and had counted over his chances for capture and escape with surprising deliberation for one who had never before been placed in so exciting and dangerous a situation. We have seen that he felt fear. Had it been otherwise he must have possessed nerves of steel, or have been utterly destitute of the power of reasoning; but that fear did not so completely overpower him as it had but a short time before, when he lay behind the bush, and listened to the guerrilla's plan for the capture of the Boxer and her crew. On the contrary, it nerved him to make the greatest exertions to effect his escape.

In a few moments, to his great joy, he emerged from the woods and entered an open field, across which he ran with redoubled speed. Directly in front of him was another belt of timber, and beyond that lay the river, which, if he could reach, he would be safe. The baying of the hound had continued to grow louder and louder, and, when Archie had accomplished perhaps half the distance across the field, a crashing in the bushes and an impatient bark announced, in language too plain to be misunderstood, that the hound had discovered him.

In an instant he stopped, faced about, and drew one of his revolvers. Stooping down close to the ground, he finally discovered the hound, which approached with loud yelps, that were answered by triumphant cheers from the pursuing rebels. Waiting until the animal was so close to him that he presented a fair mark, Archie raised his revolver and fired. The hound bounded into the air, and, after a few struggles, lay motionless on the ground. Scarcely waiting to witness the effect of the shot, the young officer sprang to his feet, and again started for the river. The yells of the rebels - who had heard the shot, and knew, from the silence that followed, that the hound was dead - again arose fierce and loud; but Archie, knowing that his pursuers had now lost the power of following him with certainty, considered the worst part of the danger as past.

But he had to deal with those who could not be easily deceived. Colonel Harrison, knowing that the only chance for escape was by the river, had lined the banks with men, and, as Archie neared the woods, a voice directly in front of him called out:

"It's all up now, Yank! Drop that shootin'-iron, or you're a gone sucker!"

Archie's heart fairly came up into his mouth. He had little expected to find an enemy in that quarter, but, without waiting an instant, he turned and ran up the river again, hoping that he might soon be able to get above the sentinels. The rebel, hearing the sound of his footsteps, and knowing that he was retreating, shouted:

"Halt, Yank! halt! or I'll shoot - blamed if I don't!"

And he *did* shoot, and Archie heard the bullet as it sung through the air behind him.

The rebel, without stopping to load his gun, started in pursuit; but Archie, who was running for his life, soon left him behind. As the latter ran he heard shots fired on all sides of him, showing that he was completely surrounded.

Escape seemed utterly impossible; and fearing that he might run into the very midst of the guerrillas when he least expected it, he threw himself behind a log in the edge of the woods, and awaited the issue of events with feelings that can not be described. He now had little hope of being able to elude his pursuers, who, he was certain, would keep the river closely guarded until daylight, when they would soon discover his hiding-place. He could not go on without fear of running against some of his enemies, in the dark, and to remain where he was, appeared equally dangerous. But of one thing he was certain - and as the thought passed through his mind, he clutched his revolvers desperately - and that was, if he was captured, it would require more than one man to do it.

Presently he heard footsteps approaching, and two rebels came up. One of them he knew, by his voice, was the very man who had just fired at him.

"I know he went this yere way," said he.

"Wal, hold on a minit," said the other, panting loudly; "let's rest a leetle - I'm nigh gin out;" and he seated himself so close to Archie that, had it been daylight, he would certainly have been discovered.

"I'll be dog-gone," said the one who had first spoken, "ef this 'ere night's work don't beat all natur'. Them ar Yanks ain't no fools, dog ef they ar!"

"Who'd a thought it?" returned his companion. "Them ar two fellers come out here an' burn a house with more'n three hundred men in it? Dog-gone! But how did that other feller get away?"

"Oh, he had a boat," answered the other, "an he got thar afore we could ketch him. He's on board his gun-boat afore this time. I jest ketched a glimpse of him as he was goin' down the bank. He had Damon by the neck, an' he was makin' him walk turkey, now I tell yer."

"Damon ketched!" ejaculated his companion. "An' what's come on the kernel's mail?"

"Gone up - the hul on it! Damon's got the bracelets on by this time. But come, let's go on."

All this while the rebels had been coming up, and Archie could hear them in the woods, on all sides of him, yelling and swearing, like demons. He had one source of consolation, however - his cousin was safe; and, judging by the rebels' conversation, he had not gone back to the vessel empty-handed.

Archie lay for some time listening to the movements of the rebels, almost afraid to breathe lest it should be overheard, when he was suddenly startled by a stunning report, which was followed by a hissing and shrieking in the air; a bright light shone in his eyes for an instant, and the next, the woods echoed with the bursting of a shell. The guerrillas had scarcely time to recover from their astonishment when there came another, and another, each one followed by groans and cries of anguish that made the young officer shudder.

Frank Nelson had gained the Boxer in safety, and although surprised and alarmed at the absence of Archie - who, he thought, would make the best of his way back to the vessel when left to himself - he knew by the yelling of the rebels, and the pistol-shots that were occasionally heard, that they had not yet captured him. The noise of the chase plainly told the Boxer's crew that the fugitive was making the best of his way up the river, and Frank had opened fire on the rebels to create, if possible, a diversion in his cousin's favor. His shells were thrown with fatal accuracy, and the guerrillas, taken completely by surprise, and having no levee to protect them, beat a hasty retreat.

Although threatened by a new danger, Archie was so overjoyed that he could scarcely refrain from shouting, and as soon as he was satisfied that his pursuers were out of hearing, he crawled from his concealment and ran toward the river. The shells still kept dropping into the woods at regular intervals, making music most pleasant to Archie's ears, for he knew that as long as the fire was continued, his chances for escape were increased. But in his eagerness he never thought of the men who had been posted on the bank, and as he dashed through the woods, several shots were fired at him by the rebels concealed in the bushes. But he reached the water in safety, and struck out for the vessel. A few random shots were fired at him, which Archie heard as they whistled past him; but his good fortune had not deserted him, and he again escaped unhurt. The reports of the guns on board the Boxer pointed out the direction in which he was to go, and in a quarter of an hour he was within hailing-distance of the vessel. The splashing he made in the water soon attracted the attention of the sentry on the forecastle, who, having been instructed by Frank, had kept a good look-out. A rope was thrown to Archie, who was pulled on board the vessel in a state of complete exhaustion.

Harry Castlemon

Frank was soon informed of the safe return of his cousin, and Archie, almost too weak to speak plainly, was carried to his room, where, after being divested of his wet clothes, he was put to bed, and left in a sound sleep. The next morning, however, he appeared in the mess-room, as lively as ever, and none the worse for his long run; while Frank, who began to suffer from his wound, was confined to his bed.

The latter listened to his cousin's narration of the part he had borne in the expedition, and in admiration of Archie's bravery, forgot the lecture he had intended to administer. The officers, who had not expected such an exhibition of courage in one whose cheek had blanched at the whistle of a rebel bullet, were astonished, and it is needless to say that no more jokes were indulged in at the expense of the "green paymaster."

For two months Frank held his position as executive officer of the Boxer, during which time the vessel was twice inspected by the admiral. He now had little to do beyond the regular routine of ship duties, for the guerrilla-station had been broken up by the burning of the plantation-house, and vessels were seldom fired into on the Boxer's beat. But this was not to continue long, for, one day, the dispatch-boat brought orders for him to report on board the Michigan - which lay at the mouth of Red River - as executive officer of that vessel.

This was still another advancement, for the Michigan was an iron-clad, mounted fourteen guns, and had a crew of one hundred and seventy men. But Frank would have preferred to remain in his present position. After considerable hard work, he had brought the Boxer's crew into an admirable state of discipline; every thing about decks went off as smoothly as could be desired, and besides, Archie was on board, and he did not wish to leave him. But he never hesitated to obey his orders, and as soon as he had packed his trunk, and taken leave of his messmates, he went on board the dispatch-boat, and in a few days arrived at his new vessel.

The captain of the Michigan had written to the admiral,

requesting that a "first-class, experienced officer" might be sent him for an executive, but when Frank presented himself and produced his orders, that gentleman was astonished. After regarding the young officer sharply for a moment, he said:

"The admiral, no doubt, knows his own business, but let me tell you, young man, that you have no easy task before you."

He no doubt thought that a person of Frank's years was utterly incapable of filling so responsible a position. The latter, with his usual modesty, replied that he would endeavor to do his duty, and after he had seen his baggage taken care of, he went into the wardroom, where he found a young officer seated at the table reading. He arose as Frank entered, and thrusting out his hand, greeted him with -

"I'm glad to meet you again, Mr. Nelson, and among friends, too."

It was George Le Dell, the escaped prisoner, whom he had met during his memorable flight from Shreveport. Frank had not seen him, nor even heard of him, since he had left him on board the Ticonderoga; but here he was, "among the defenders of the Old Flag" again, in fulfillment of the promise he had made his rebel father, in the letter which Frank had read to his fellow fugitives in the woods, where they had halted for the day. He was not changed - his face still wore that sorrowful expression - and Frank found that he rarely took part in the conversation around the mess-table. He was an excellent officer, the especial favorite of the captain, and beloved by all his messmates, who, very far from suspecting the cause of his quiet demeanor, called him "Silence."

Frank heartily returned his cordial greeting, and the two friends talked for a long time of scenes through which they had passed together - subjects still fresh in their memories - until the entrance of an officer put a stop to the conversation. Frank understood, by this, that he was the only one of the ship's company who knew any thing of George's past history.

The change from the cool, comfortable quarters of the Boxer to the hot wardroom of the ironclad was not an agreeable one; but Frank was not the one to complain, and he entered upon his duties with his accustomed cheerfulness and alacrity. He was allowed very little rest. The captain of the Michigan - which was the flag-ship of the third division of the squadron - was a regular officer, who believed in always keeping the men busy at something, and Frank was obliged to be on his feet from morning until night. The decks were scrubbed every day, the bright work about the guns and engines cleaned, the small boats washed out, and then came quarters, and drilling with muskets or broad-swords. After this, if there was nothing else to be done, the outside of the vessel was scrubbed, or the chimneys repainted. In short, the Michigan was the pattern of neatness, and her crew, being constantly drilled, knew exactly what was required of them, and were ready for any emergency.

For several months little occurred to relieve the monotony of ship-life beyond making regular trips from one end of their beat to the other; but when spring opened, gun-boats and transports, loaded with soldiers, began to assemble, and preparations were made for the Red River expedition. At length every thing was ready, and one pleasant morning the gun-boats weighed their anchors and led the way up the river.

Frank stood on deck as the vessels steamed along, and could not help drawing a contrast between his present position and the one in which he was placed when he first saw Red River. Then, he and his companions were fugitives from a rebel prison; they had been tracked by bloodhounds, and followed by men at whose hands, if retaken, they could expect nothing but death. He remembered how his heart bounded with joy on the morning when he and his associates, in their leaky dug-out, had arrived in sight of the Mississippi. Then, he was ragged, hatless, and almost shoeless, weary with watching, and living in constant fear of recapture. Now, he was among friends, the Old Flag waved above him, and he was the second in command of one of the finest vessels in the squadron.

The passage up the river was without incident worthy of note, and in a short time they arrived at the obstructions which the rebels had placed in the river nine miles below Fort De Russy. A vast amount of time and labor had been expended upon these obstructions, but they were speedily cleared away, and the fleet passed on. They had expected a stubborn resistance at the fort, but it had been captured by the army after a short engagement, and the gun-boats kept on to Alexandria.

CHAPTER VI

FRANK TURNS DETECTIVE

A day or two after the arrival of the fleet at Alexandria, it became known that several persons belonging to the rebel secret service were hovering about in the vicinity of the village, with the intention of destroying some of the vessels by torpedoes - contrivances made to resemble pieces of coal - which were to be placed in those barges out of which the boats were supplied with fuel. By some means the names of these persons became known to the admiral, who issued a general order, calling on all the officers of the squadron to kill or capture them wherever found.

The same day the order was issued Frank obtained shore liberty, and while roaming about the town, espied a name on a sign that immediately attracted his attention. It was one of the names borne in the general order.

"There's one of the rascals, now," soliloquized Frank, "or, rather, where he has been. I wonder where he is. I'll see if I can't find out something about him. If he could be caught, he would be put in a place where he wouldn't lay any more plans to blow up Union gun-boats."

The sign which had attracted his attention bore the name and occupation of the individual in question - "S. W. ABBOTT, Chemist."

The store had been closed on the approach of the Union forces, and was now in the possession of several army surgeons and their assistants, who were overhauling its contents, and appropriating whatever they thought might be of service to them. A negro was leaning against the counter, and of him Frank inquired -

"Boy, do you belong here?"

"No, sar," he answered, indignantly; "I 'longs nowhar. I'se a free man, I is. I'se a soger."

"Never been in this town before?"

"No, sar."

Frank left the store, and walked slowly up the street toward the hotel, wondering where he could go to make inquiries concerning the man whom he wished to find. It was evident that this was the hardest task he had yet undertaken. He knew the rebel's name, and that was all. He had no idea how he looked, and, although the admiral's order stated that he was loitering about the village, he might, at that moment, be fifty miles away, or Frank might have already passed him on the street.

There were several men dressed in butternut clothes hanging about the hotel, and Frank determined to enter into conversation with one of them, and, if possible, learn something about Abbott. An opportunity was soon offered, for one of the butternuts approached him, and inquired -

"Got any Northern money - greenbacks?"

"Some," replied Frank.

"Wal," continued the man, "I'll give you five dollars in Confederate money fur one dollar in greenbacks. Is it a bargain?"

"Confederate money!" repeated Frank. "Of what use would it be to me? And I am greatly mistaken if it will be of use to you much longer."

"Wal, I want your money fur a keepsake," replied the man. I know you-uns don't like our money, but we-uns hev got to use it or go without any,"

"Well, I'll trade," said Frank. "Your paper will no doubt be a curiosity to the folks at home." As he spoke, he produced the dollar, and the butternut drew out of his capacious pocket a huge roll of bills - tens, twenties, and fifties, enough to have made him independent if it had been good money - and selecting a five-dollar bill, handed it to Frank, who thrust it carelessly into his pocket.

"I'll allow that you-uns don't seem to be a bad lot of fellers," said the butternut; "but I don't see what you-uns want to come down hyar to fight we-uns for. We-uns never done nothing to you-uns."

"Every rebel I meet says the same thing," said Frank. "But who were the richest men in this place before the war broke out?"

The man mentioned several names, among which was that of Abbott, the chemist.

"Abbott, Abbott," repeated Frank, as if trying to recall the man to mind; "I've heard that name before. Is he a Northern man?"

"No; he's allers lived at the South. His house is right back of the hotel, third door from the corner, on the right-hand side as you go up the street."

Frank had learned something, but he did not think it safe to question the man further, for fear of exciting his suspicions; so, after a few unimportant remarks, he turned on his heel and walked into the hotel, which was used as the army head-quarters. Here he remained for nearly half an hour, to give the man of whom he had received his information time to leave the place, and then directed his steps toward Mr. Abbott's dwelling. He had no difficulty in finding it, for he followed the butternut's directions, and the rebel's name was borne on the door-plate. The house, however, was deserted; the blinds were closed, as were those of all the neighboring houses. Mr. Abbott, with his family, if he had any, had doubtless removed out of reach of the Union forces. Did he ever visit his home when in town? or did he make his head-quarters somewhere else? were questions that suggested themselves to Frank, but which, of course, he could not answer; neither did he dare to question any of the citizens, for they might be Mr. Abbott's friends, who would not fail to inform him that particular inquiries were being made, which would lead him to act more cautiously. Frank did not know what plan to adopt, but walked listlessly about the streets until he heard the Michigan's bell strike half-past three o'clock. He must be on board by four, as the admiral was to be there to inspect the vessel. He was reluctant to leave without having accomplished any thing more than the discovery of the rebel's dwelling; but there was no help for it, and he walked slowly toward the landing, where he found a boat waiting for him.

That night, although he retired early, he slept but little, but tossed restlessly about in his bunk, endeavoring to conjure up some plan by which he might capture the rebel; and when he fell asleep, he dreamed about the subject uppermost in his mind. He thought that, after several days' patient watching, he finally discovered his man; but all attempts to capture him were unavailing. When he pursued, the rebel would disappear in a magical way, that was perfectly bewildering. Finally, he dreamed that the rebel assumed the offensive, and one day he met him in the street, carrying in his hand something that looked like a lump of coal, which he threw at Frank. It proved, however, to be a torpedo, for it exploded with a loud report, and as Frank sprang over a fence that ran close by the sidewalk, to escape, he came violently in contact with the walls of a house. At this stage of his dream he was suddenly awakened. To his no small amazement, he found himself stretched on the floor of his room, his head jammed against the door, through which one of the wardroom boys, a very small specimen of a contraband, was endeavoring to escape, while the look of terror depicted on his face, and the energy with which he strove to open the door, showed that he had sustained something of a fright. On the opposite side of the room stood the doctor, who gazed at Frank for a moment with open mouth and eyes, and then threw himself on the bed, convulsed with laughter.

Frank rose slowly to his feet, and commenced drawing on his clothes, while the little negro disappeared through the door like a flash.

"Mr. Nelson," said the doctor, as soon as he could speak, "you can't make that jump again, sir. I came in to awaken you," he continued, "and was just going to put my hand on you, when you sprang out of your bunk upon your trunk, and then back again; and just as the darkey was coming in, you made another jump, and landed against the door, frightening him so that I actually believe he turned pale. Were you dreaming?"

"Yes," answered Frank, with a laugh; "I was getting out of the way of a torpedo."

"Well, you certainly jumped far enough to get out of the way of almost any thing," replied the doctor, after he had indulged in another hearty fit of laughter. "Hurry up; breakfast is nearly ready."

Frank felt the effects of his agility in the shape of a severe pain over his left eye, which had been occasioned by his head coming in contact with the door-knob, and his "big jump" was the source of a good deal of merriment at the breakfast-table.

Frank went ashore in the ten-o'clock boat, and, after strolling about with his companions for a short time, invented a satisfactory excuse for his absence, and started toward Mr. Abbott's house, which, to his joy, he found open, with a negro engaged in sweeping the steps.

"Boy, who lives here?" he inquired.

The negro gave the desired information, adding: "He ain't hyar though, but missus will be home dis arternoon."

"Where's your master?"

"Oh, he done gone off somewhar. I 'spects he don't like for to see you Yankee sogers hyar."

As the negro ceased speaking, having finished his work, he turned and went into the house, while Frank was about to move away, wondering what was the next thing to be done, when a boy approached and opened the gate.

"What do you want?" asked Frank.

The boy held up a letter which he carried in his hand, and Frank, seeing that it was addressed to Mrs. Abbott, at once concluded that it contained information which might be of the greatest value to him.

"It is all right," said he; "I'll attend to it;" at the same time taking the note and handing some money to the boy, who departed well satisfied. Frank then walked down the street, and, as soon as he was out of sight of the house, opened the letter and read as follows:

HEYWARD'S PLANTATION, *March* 20, 1864.

"Will be at home at eight o'clock this evening. Have my baggage ready to start for Shreveport early in the morning."

No name was signed to the note, but Frank was certain that he now had the matter in his own hands, and that any preparations Mrs. Abbott might make for her husband's journey to Shreveport would only be thrown away. He at once directed his steps toward the landing, hailed his vessel for a boat, and when he had arrived on board and reported to the captain, showed that gentleman the note, at the same time requesting permission to remain on shore after dark, in order to capture the rebel.

"I should be only too happy to allow you to do so, Mr. Nelson," said the captain, "for you seem to be particularly fortunate in every thing of this description you undertake. But, as it is the admiral's order that all officers repair on board their vessels at sundown, he must be consulted in regard to the matter. Orderly, tell the officer of the deck to have the gig called away. We will go up to the flag-ship," he continued, "and talk to the admiral."

The gig was soon manned, and after Frank had buckled on his sword (for all officers visiting the flag-ship were required to wear their side-arms), he stepped into the boat with the captain, and in a short time they were in the presence of the admiral. The captain, in a few words, explained the nature of the visit, showed him the note Frank had intercepted, and ended by repeating the young officer's request that he might be allowed to remain on shore after dark.

"Certainly," replied the admiral, "certainly. If you succeed, young man, we shall have one less of these secret-service fellows to fear." Then, turning to one of his clerks, he gave him an order which Frank did not hear, after which he asked:

"How did you discover the whereabouts of this man Abbott, Mr. Nelson?"

Frank then proceeded to give the admiral an account of all he had done, how he had seen the rebel's name on the sign, learned his residence, and secured the note. To all of which the latter listened with attention.

"I hope you will succeed in capturing him," said he. "If you do, bring him here; I want a look at him. Here," he continued, as his clerk handed him a letter, "is a request that the provost-marshal will furnish you with a pass. Good luck to you, young man."

Their business being finished, Frank followed the captain out of the cabin, and returned on board the Michigan.

All that afternoon Frank was in a fever of excitement. He was impatient for the night to come, that he might know whether or not his attempt was to be crowned with success. A hundred things might happen to prevent it. The rebel might not come home, or the note might have been written with the intention of having it intercepted, in order to throw the one into whose hands it might fall on the wrong scent; or it might be written in cipher, and mean directly opposite to what Frank had supposed. But he consoled himself with the thought that he had done, and would still continue to do, all in his power to obey the admiral's general order, and if he failed, the blame would not rest with him.

When the sundown boat was called away, Frank, after exchanging his uniform for a citizen's dress, and his cap for a tattered slouch-hat, thrust a revolver into his pocket, stepped into the cutter, and was soon set on shore. He walked directly to the office of the provost-marshal, which was in the hotel, and finding that officer at his desk, handed him the admiral's note, which ran as follows:

> "U. S. FLAG-SHIP BLACKHAWK,
> "OFF ALEXANDRIA, LA., March 20, 1864.

"SIR: - Please furnish the bearer, Acting Ensign Frank Nelson, with a pass. He has important business to perform, which may detain him on shore most of the night, and it is absolutely necessary, for the successful accomplishment of his mission, that he should not be interfered with.

Very respectfully, your obd't serv't.,

> DAVID D. PORTER, *Rear Admiral*,
> Com'd'g Miss. Squadron.

U. S. Provost Marshal,
Alexandria, La.

"Your business must be important indeed, judging by the language of this note," said the marshal. "You shall not be troubled."

While he was speaking he had been writing an order commanding "all guards and patrols to allow the bearer the freedom of the city, as he was under special orders from the admiral, and must not be detained."

"There," said he, after he had finished the pass and handed it to Frank. "That will take you through all right. You have my best wishes for your success."

Frank thanked him, and putting the pass carefully away in his pocket, walked out of the hotel fully satisfied on one point, and that was, if his success depended upon the good wishes of his friends, failure was impossible. He walked slowly down the street toward the place where the soldiers were encamped; for as it lacked fully an hour and a half of the appointed time, he did not wish to be seen loitering about the house, as it might excite the suspicions of its inmates, who would not fail to send word to Mr. Abbott that the house was being watched. Time moved altogether too slowly for the impatient young officer, but at length he heard the flag-ship's bell strike half-past seven, and as it had begun to grow dark, he walked toward the house, and took his station in the shadow of some trees on the opposite side of the street. At the end of an hour his patience was rewarded, for he heard the sound of approaching footsteps, and a man passed by the house. Frank knew, from the suspicious manner in which he gazed about, that if it was not the man for whom he was waiting, it was some other guilty fellow who ought to be secured. Presently he returned, and after again looking cautiously about him, ascended the steps and knocked lightly at the door, which was almost instantly opened, and a voice exclaimed:

"Massa Abbott, I'se glad to" -

The rest of the sentence Frank did not hear, for the moment the man entered the hall, the door was closed again. Now was the time for Frank, who hastily crossed the street, and noiselessly ascended the steps. Here he paused for a moment to draw his revolver, and then suddenly opened the door and sprang into the hall. He was met by the negro, the same, no doubt, whom he had heard welcoming his master, who, not liking the looks of the huge six-shooter which the officer flourished before his eyes, beat a hasty retreat. Frank kept on and entered the parlor, where he found his man standing in the middle of the floor, pale and breathless. No one else was in the room.

"Mr. Abbott," said Frank, "you're my prisoner!"

The man, who was so terrified that he seemed to have lost even the power of speech, surrendered his weapons and submitted to his captor, who led him out of the house and toward the flag-ship, which they reached in safety. The admiral received Frank with great cordiality, and after listening to his account of the manner in which the capture of the prisoner had been effected, he ordered the cutter called away, and the young officer, rejoicing over his success, was sent on board his vessel.

CHAPTER VII

FRANK'S FIRST COMMAND

The next morning, just after quarters, while the officers were getting ready to go on shore, a boat from the flag-ship came alongside, and the officer in charge of it was shown into the cabin, as he said he had business with the captain. Frank, who thought he had accomplished sufficient to satisfy him to remain on board, sat in the wardroom reading, when the orderly entered and informed him that the captain desired his presence in the cabin.

"Mr. Nelson," said he, "here's an order from the admiral, directing me to furnish you with a cutter and an armed crew, and to send you to the flag-ship for orders. I am also instructed to appoint an executive to fill your place during your absence. I expect you will be sent off on some expedition; so you had better prepare for a long trip."

The officer who brought the order having returned to his vessel, the captain accompanied Frank on deck, and ordered the second cutter to be called away and furnished with a crew well armed. In a short time the boat was ready, and Frank, buckling on his side-arms, took leave of the captain and started toward the flag-ship, wondering what duty he was now called upon to perform, and fully determined that whatever orders he might receive, however dangerous or difficult, should be executed, if within the bounds of possibility.

When he arrived on board the Blackhawk, an officer, who appeared to be waiting for him, conducted him into the cabin, where the admiral sat writing at his desk.

"Good morning, Mr. Nelson," said he; "take a chair, sir."

Frank took the seat pointed out to him, and the admiral, taking from his desk a bundle of papers, carefully tied up, continued:

"It has always been my habit, Mr. Nelson, not to let a brave or skillful action pass unrewarded, any more than I would allow a bad one to pass unpunished. I am now about to give you a much more important, and perhaps dangerous, commission than has yet been intrusted to you. This package contains official documents of the greatest importance, and I want you to go down the river, and deliver it to the commanding naval officer, whom you will find at Acklen's plantation, opposite the mouth of Red River. I know there are rebels all along the banks, but whatever you do, don't allow these letters to fall into their hands. There are iron weights in the package, and if you should be in danger of capture, throw it overboard. You will take passage on the army transport that now lies at the stern of this vessel, all ready to start. I send the cutter and armed crew with you, for the reason that the rebels may sink the transport, in which case you can escape in your boat; for those letters must go through, if possible; perhaps the success of this expedition depends upon them. The transport, you will find, is in command of a second-lieutenant. I should feel much safer if I could put one of my own officers in charge, but, as the boat belongs to the army, I have no authority in the matter. After you have executed your orders, return, by first opportunity, to your vessel, and report to me by letter. Now, sir, you may go, for they are waiting for you. Remember, I say the success or failure of this entire expedition may depend upon you; and don't forget that you are the young man that saved the Milwaukee."

Frank bowed himself out of the cabin, sprang into the cutter, and started toward the transport that lay alongside of the bank, a short distance below the flag-ship. As he stepped on board, he was met by a flashy-looking young lieutenant, dressed in a brand-new uniform, who greeted him with the inquiry:

"Are you ready at last? I have been waiting an hour for you. Business is business, you know, and when I command a ship, I don't like to be detained."

The lieutenant said this, probably, to impress upon Frank's mind the important fact that he was the captain of the steamer, and must be respected and obeyed accordingly. Frank, who knew that he was not subject to the orders of the lieutenant only so far as the safety of the vessel was concerned, replied that he had come as soon as he could after he had received his orders, and turning to his men, directed part of them to make the cutter fast to the stern of the steamer, and the others to carry their arms to the boiler-deck, where they could be readily seized in case of emergency. The transport was a small side-wheel boat belonging to the quarter-master's department. The deck-hands were all soldiers - perhaps half a dozen of them in all - the only steamboatmen on board being one pilot, four engineers, and as many firemen. The steamer was armed with two howitzers, mounted on the boiler-deck, and the muskets of the soldiers were stacked in the cabin. The boilers were protected by bales of cotton, which were piled on the guards, and the pilot-house was defended in the same manner. A few bales were also placed on the boiler-deck to serve as a breastwork. The whole was under the command of the lieutenant, who, judging by the orders he issued, knew nothing whatever of the management of a boat.

Frank had been on board but a few moments, when the engineer's bell rang, to inform the pilot that all was ready for the start. The boat was made fast by a single line, which ran from the forecastle to a tree on the bank, and the gang-plank was out. The lieutenant's first order was, "Haul in that plank." The soldiers obeyed, and then came the command for "somebody to run out there and untie that line."

One of the soldiers sprang ashore and began trying to cast off the line, which was drawn as taut as a four-mile current could make it. He worked for several moments, but, of course without success (for the line should first have been slackened up on board), and then called out:

"Loosen up that other end, there!"

"No, no!" replied the lieutenant, "that would allow the boat to swing away from the bank, and then how would you get on board? It must be untied from that tree first."

What difference it could possibly make in regard to the boat's swinging away from the bank, whether the line was first slackened up on shore or on board, Frank could not determine.

He was astonished at the lieutenant's ignorance, and amused at his novel mode of casting off a line, while the sailors, who had gathered in a group on the forecastle, watched the operation with a smile, wondering how the affair would end, as they knew that the line could not be "untied" from the tree unless first slackened up on board. But the lieutenant seemed to have his own idea of the manner in which it ought to be accomplished, and was constantly ordering the man to "Hurry up, there!" The soldiers worked and pulled, but all to no purpose, and the lieutenant, becoming impatient, ordered two more of the men to his assistance. But the knot, which had been awkwardly made, was jammed, and resisted their utmost efforts.

"I never did see such a clumsy set of fellows," said the lieutenant, at length, turning to Frank, who stood beside him, making use of his handkerchief to conceal his laughter. "We ought to have been two miles down the river by this time."

It was evident that he was fast becoming disgusted with his first attempt at "steamboating," but was too proud to ask advice. At length he turned and walked into the cabin, muttering, "I guess they will get it untied before night." But Frank was unwilling to wait so long. The delay was entirely unnecessary, and he had begun to get impatient.

"Men," said he, addressing himself to the cutter's crew, who were convulsed with laughter, "some of you run out that gang-plank, and another slack up that line."

These orders were promptly obeyed, and the difficulty was easily overcome.

"All gone, sir," shouted Frank to the pilot, meaning that the line was cast off, and in a few moments the transport swung off from the bank, and was plowing her way down the river. Frank leaned over the railing, and wondered how a man so utterly ignorant of the management of a steamer, as was the lieutenant, came to be put in command, and at a time, too, when they might be placed in situations that would call into requisition all the skill and judgment of experienced men. He did not at all like the appearance of the young commander, for he was of the type of officers known as "upstarts," who like to show their authority, but are without the ability to successfully fill even the post of corporal. What if the transport should be fired upon and disabled? It was evident that in such an emergency nothing could be expected of a man who could not cast off a line. Frank's commission was too important to be intrusted to the care of such a man, and the young officer felt that he would much rather step into the cutter, and trust to the skill and courage of his twelve sailors, than to remain on board the transport. Calling the coxswain on deck, he directed that if they were attacked, the cutter should be kept ready for instant use, and in case the vessel was disabled, they would attempt to finish their journey in her. After giving these orders, Frank went up into the pilot-house, where he found the man at the wheel in no enviable state of mind.

"I'm glad to see you," said he, as Frank entered, "for I want to talk to you. I'm not at all pleased with the looks of our skipper," he went on to say, "and how he came to be placed in command is a mystery to me. Perhaps the quarter-master thinks, like a good many men who see the Mississippi River for the first time, that any body can take charge of a steamboat; but suppose we should run aground - what does that lieutenant know about sparring off? or what if something about the engine should let down? why, we might go forty miles down the river before he could get us tied up to the bank. Besides, if we are fired upon, he'll surrender. Now, mark my words, he'll surrender before he will fight, and I'm opposed to that, for I was a prisoner once."

"So was I," said Frank, "and I don't mean to fall into the rebels' hands again, if I can help it. I'll never be surrendered. That lieutenant may not fight, but I think his men will, and I have twelve good fellows, all well armed, on whom I know I can depend."

"Then I feel better," said the pilot. "That's talk I like to hear; for if we are not disabled, we'll go through all right. There goes the bell! Go down and get your dinner."

Frank deposited his weapons on a bench in the pilot-house and ran down into the cabin, where he found the lieutenant and two engineers seated at the table. The former seemed to have forgotten his failure of the morning, for he talked a good deal in a condescending manner, as if addressing his inferiors; and to Frank's inquiry if he expected trouble from the rebels, replied that he had not given the matter a moment's thought; that if they did attack the vessel, it would not be the first time he had smelt powder, and if the engineers and pilot could be depended upon, he had no fears but that he should be able to take the boat safely through. Frank replied that he trusted the officers would not be found wanting in courage; and when he had finished his meal, he went on deck again, and surprised the pilot, by offering to relieve him while he went down to his dinner. In his spare moments Frank, who wisely regarded it as the duty of every officer to acquaint himself with every part of the management of a vessel, had learned to handle the wheel, and he was an excellent steersman. He could make a landing or get a boat under way, as well as the most experienced pilot; and in the present instance he was fully capable of steering the boat, for as the water in the river was high, there was no danger of getting out of the channel.

The pilot gave him his place, and after watching the movements of the young officer, who handled the wheel with all the confidence of an old river man, he went below to his dinner, satisfied that he had left the boat in safe hands. Frank remained at the wheel most of the afternoon, for the pilot, who would be on watch all night, had gone to bed to obtain a few hours' rest. About four o'clock, however, he made his appearance, and Frank went down into the cabin, and was engaged in reading a, newspaper, when he heard the pilot shout through the trumpet to the engineers:

"Here they are! Now, push her ahead strong. There's a battery just below."

At the same moment there was a rush of feet on deck, and the lieutenant entered the cabin pale and breathless.

"We're captured," said he, in a faint voice. "We're surrounded. The bank is black with rebels - ten thousand of them at least! It's no use to think of fighting."

As he ceased speaking, he ran on deck again, followed by Frank, who found his men drawn up behind the cotton-bales, with their weapons in their hands, waiting for orders. The soldiers had cast loose the howitzers, and stood at their posts. The lieutenant stopped a moment, just long enough to say, "Boys, we're all captured!" and then ran into the pilot-house. As Frank stood talking to his men, and encouraging them with the famous words that never fail to nerve an American seaman - "Don't give up the ship!" - a rebel rode out on the bank, in full view of the steamer, and shouted:

"Come ashore here, or we'll sink you."

Frank looked toward the pilot-house, where the lieutenant had taken refuge, and waited to hear his answer. To his surprise and horror, he saw a hand extended waving a white handkerchief, and the coxswain exclaimed:

"Mr. Nelson, he's surrendering us, sir!"

With one bound Frank sprang up the steps that led to the pilot-house, caught the handkerchief and threw it overboard; and at the same moment the lieutenant was seized from behind and thrown to the deck. He instantly recovered his feet, and turning fiercely upon Frank and the pilot, exclaimed:

"What are you about? Do you know that you have rendered yourselves liable to a court-martial? I'm commander of this vessel, and I'll shoot the first man that resists my authority!"

"You shall never surrender us," said Frank, firmly, not the least intimidated by the other's threat. "If you will give orders for your men to prepare for action, no one will oppose you. We'll stick to you as long as a plank of this vessel remains above water."

"I know my own business," replied the lieutenant. "Resistance is useless. We never could get by that battery, and I'm going to surrender to save our lives. Turn her toward the shore, pilot!"

As he spoke, he walked out on deck, and calling out to the rebel, who had continued to follow the vessel:

"I'll surrender! Pilot, I tell you to turn her in toward the shore."

The pilot gave a glance at Frank, and reading in his face a firm determination to go through if possible, held the boat's head down the stream, while a murmur of indignation arose from the men on the lower deck, and the coxswain said, turning to his companions:

"Sink my tarry wig, if that ar' chap ain't going to give us up without our having the least bit of a fight."

Frank stood for a moment irresolute. Ought he to oppose the lieutenant, the lawful commander of the vessel? Was it his duty to stand by and allow himself and his men to be surrendered without even a show of resistance? And his dispatches, the importance of which the admiral had stated in such emphatic language, should he throw them overboard, instead of delivering them, as he had hoped to do, to the officer to whom they were addressed? No! Sooner than do that, he would put the cowardly lieutenant under arrest, and give the command to the pilot, a man whom he knew understood his business, and would not think of surrender until it had been clearly proved that successful resistance was entirely out of the question.

While these thoughts were passing through Frank's mind, the boat, under an increased head of steam, had been rapidly nearing the battery, which could be distinctly seen about half a mile below, planted on the bank of the river.

"Come ashore, if you surrender," shouted the rebel.

"Pilot," said the lieutenant, in a weak voice, "I order you" -

He never finished that order, for Frank seized him, and pulling him into the pilot-house, closed the door. He made an attempt to draw a revolver, but the pilot threw him to the deck, when Frank wrested the weapon from him and retained it in his possession.

"All ready forward there?" he shouted to the men on the boiler-deck.

"Ay, ay, sir," answered the coxswain. "Mr. Nelson's in command," he added, turning to his companions. "Douse my to'-gallant top-lights but we'll have a skirmish now sure."

"Do you surrender?" shouted the man on the bank.

The reply he received was a shot from the pilot's revolver, which made him beat a hasty retreat. He had scarcely disappeared when a cloud of men arose from behind the levee, and a volley of bullets rattled into the boat. It was answered by a shout of defiance from the men behind the cotton-bales; but the pilot, who stood just in front of Frank, staggered for a moment, and sank heavily to the deck. Frank was horrified. With that man at the wheel, he had entertained no fears of their ability to run by the battery; but now that he was left alone, with the duties of both commander and pilot devolving upon him, his hopes fell again. But he could not remain long inactive, for the boat, being without a guide, began to swing toward the shore. Hastily seizing the wheel, he turned her head down the river again, when the battery opened upon them, and a storm of shells plunged into the water and whistled through the air about the boat. Only one struck her, and that passed through one of the smoke-stacks, and bursting, demolished part of the roof of the pilothouse. Then, as fast as the guns could be loaded, the battery played upon the transport, and Frank heard the shells crashing through the cabin and exploding in the air above him. But he stood bravely at his post, his only fears being of his inability to turn the point on which the battery was planted, or that one of the shells might penetrate the cotton-bales and strike the boilers or some part of the machinery. But as he neared the battery, he discovered that the boat was struck less frequently; that the rebels, in their excitement, were firing wildly. His own men, cool and collected, encouraged by the example of their officer, had not yet fired a shot; but when the boat arrived opposite the battery, they opened upon it with the howitzers and small arms with terrible effect. The point, which extended into the bend where the battery stood, was long and sharp, a bad place for one unaccustomed to handling a boat; but Frank passed it in safety, under a full head of steam, and cheers of triumph arose from his men, which the rebels answered with yells of rage, and continued to follow the transport, sending bullets and shells after her as fast as they could reload. But they were speedily left behind, and their yells died away in the distance.

Frank's dispatches were safe.

CHAPTER VIII

AN UNLUCKY FIGHT

As soon as Frank was certain that the rebels had given up the pursuit, he called two of his men on deck, and directed them to carry the pilot, who now began to show signs of returning consciousness, into the cabin.

During the fight the lieutenant had remained behind one of the cotton-bales, where the pilot had thrown him, so completely overcome with fear that he did not think of renewing his attempts to enforce his authority. But now that the danger was over, he arose to his feet and walked out of the pilot-house. As the sailors came up, in obedience to Frank's order, they passed the lieutenant without giving the customary salute, and acted as though they considered him beneath their notice. They lifted the pilot tenderly in their arms, carried him down stairs, and laid him on his bed.

There was no surgeon on board, and Frank was anxious to reach a gun-boat as soon as possible, in order to place the pilot, who was the only one injured, under the care of a medical man. He kept his place at the wheel, his supper being brought up to him by one of his men, and shortly after dark came within sight of the lights of a vessel which was lying at anchor in the stream. He blew the whistle, to let her know that he was approaching, to which the steamer, which proved to be a gun-boat, replied by hoisting her signal-lights. Frank having no signals, whistled again, and rang the bells for the engineer to run slowly. As soon as he came within hailing distance, a voice called out:

"Steamer ahoy!"

"Ay, ay, sir!" shouted Frank, in reply.

"What steamer is that?"

"Army transport Key-West, bound for the mouth of the river, with dispatches from the admiral."

"Come alongside, here," shouted the voice.

"Ay, ay, sir," replied Frank, and he commenced turning the boat's head toward the vessel, while a hurrying of feet and a noise of dropping handspikes on the gun-deck, told him in plain language that the captain of the gun-boat was not at all satisfied with the report he had made, and had called his crew to quarters, to be in readiness to sink the transport if she should attempt to run by. It was an uncommon thing during the expedition for boats to run in Red River after night, unless supplied with the necessary signals, and the young officer was not at all surprised at the precautions taken by the gun-boat.

Frank by this time had turned the transport around, and was coming up at the stern of the gun-boat, when the lieutenant came on deck, and entering the pilot-house, inquired:

"Are you the captain of this ship?"

"I have had no orders to act as such," replied Frank.

"Then why do you answer hails, and land here without my permission? I'll have you court-martialed."

"I answered the hails because you were not on deck; and I land here because I have been ordered to do so by the captain of that gun-boat."

"Well, I am not under his orders; he has no authority over me, and I order you to turn around at once, and start down the river again."

"If I should undertake that," replied Frank, with a laugh, "this vessel wouldn't last long. Every cannon on this aide of that gun-boat points straight at us, and if we should turn around, they would blow us out of water."

"They would, eh?" said the lieutenant, angrily. "I'll have the whole lot of them up before a court-martial. I'm a second-lieutenant, sir, and must not be detained, as I am on important business. Turn around at once."

Frank made no reply, and at that moment the bow of the transport touched the gun-boat, and one of the sailors sprang out with a line. As soon as the boat was made fast, he put on his side-arms, and taking his dispatches, walked out of the pilot-house, leaving the lieutenant almost beside himself with rage. As soon as he stepped on board the gun-boat, he was shown into the presence of Captain Wilson, the same who had commanded the Ticonderoga when Frank was attached to her.

"Oh, is it you, Mr. Nelson?" he exclaimed, seizing the young officer's hand and shaking it heartily. "Then it's all right. I did not know but you were a rebel, and were going to run by; so I got my guns all ready to sink you. Sit down. Are you in command?"

Frank replied that he was not, and then proceeded to repeat the orders he had received from the admiral, telling the captain of the fight with the battery, but carefully omitting any thing that related to the conduct of the lieutenant, he ended by saying that the pilot was wounded, and requesting that the doctor might be sent on board to attend to him, which was done at once, the captain offering to send another pilot to take his place.

The transport lay alongside nearly two hours, during which

time the pilot's wound, which was not dangerous, was dressed. The doctor then declared that he was able to go on to the mouth of the river, where he could be placed under the care of an army surgeon. Frank then took his leave of the captain, and stepped on board the transport, accompanied by one of the gun-boat pilots, who was well-known to the young officer, and he was confident that the lieutenant, if he should again take it into his head to give any unnecessary orders, would hear the truth plainly told. He was an old acquaintance of the wounded pilot, from whom he had heard the whole history of the trip from Alexandria; but as he had said nothing about the matter to Frank, the latter was not aware that he knew it.

The pilot took his station at the wheel, while Frank seated himself on the boiler-deck railing. The lieutenant stood close by, and, without waiting to hear whether or not the engineers were ready to start, shouted:

"Untie that line."

"Hold on!" shouted the pilot. "Do you want to send us adrift without any steam? Wait till I tell you we're all ready."

The engineers of the transport, taking advantage of the landing, had allowed the steam to go down, in order to repair some part of the machinery that was out of order, and had the line been cast off just then, the boat would have been at the mercy of the current, and in danger of sinking, for a short distance below lay an iron-clad ram, anchored in the river. The lieutenant had given his command in a loud tone, in order to be heard by the crew of the gun-boat, and the rebuff he had met from the pilot did not tend to quiet his feelings, which were considerably agitated by the thought that he was not in reality the commander of the vessel. He was astonished at the pertinacity with which his subordinates (as he considered them) countermanded his orders, and wondered what was the use of being captain of a vessel if he was not to be obeyed. But perhaps the new pilot did not know who he was. He would inform him. With this determination, he walked up to the pilot-house, and inquired:

"Do you know, sir, that I command this boat?"

"Yes," replied the pilot, "I know all about that. But you had better go and turn in; you are only in the way here. All ready, Mr. Nelson," he continued, as the engineer's bell rang at this moment.

Frank gave the necessary orders, and in a few moments they were again on their way down the river, while the lieutenant walked into the cabin and threw himself on a lounge, heartily wishing there were no gun-boat men in existence. As soon as they were fairly under way, Frank, seeing that the lieutenant took no further notice of what was going on, ran below to set the watch; then, after satisfying himself that every thing was right about decks, and that their weapons were ready for instant use, he stretched himself on a blanket in the cabin, and with his precious dispatches (which he had carried with him wherever he went) for a pillow, was soon fast asleep.

About midnight he was suddenly awakened by a terrific crash, and sprang to his feet to find the cabin shrouded in darkness and filled with smoke. Hastily thrusting his dispatches into his pocket, he commenced groping for his side-arms, which, on retiring, he had placed by his side, while a commotion on deck told him that the crew were hurrying to their stations. When he had found his sword, he ran out of the cabin, and saw his men drawn up behind the cotton-bales, under charge of the coxswain, who ran up to his officer and hurriedly asked for orders. The latter did not long remain ignorant of the nature of the attack, for a shell plunged into the cabin which he had just left, and, exploding with a deafening report, filled the air with fragments of furniture, and tore a large hole in the deck above the boilers. The night was very dark, but still there was light enough for Frank to see that the boat, no longer obeying her helm, was drifting broadside toward the battery, the position of which could be easily determined by the flash of its guns; and it was evident that unless those guns could be speedily silenced, the transport would be altogether demolished, or disabled so that she would fall into the hands of the rebels. Turning to the oxswain, Frank inquired:

"Is that cutter ready for immediate use?"

"All ready, sir," was the answer.

"Let loose those guns, then. Fire!"

The two howitzers belched forth their contents, but while they were being reloaded, another broadside from the battery plunged into the boat, followed by the hissing and shrieking of steam. A shot had struck the boilers! The thought had scarcely passed through Frank's mind, when the pilot sprang down the steps, exclaiming:

"Mr. Nelson, the tiller-rope is shot away, sir, and the boat is on fire!"

In short, much sooner than Frank had expected, the transport was a complete wreck.

The cotton-bales on the guards had been set on fire by a bursting shell; the tiller-rope shot away, rendering it impossible to steer the boat; the boilers penetrated, and the engine-room filled with hot steam, which now began to rise and envelop the men on the boiler-deck. Soldiers and sailors at once deserted their quarters and ran about in confusion, while Frank, with his handkerchief in his mouth, to prevent his inhaling the steam, stood wondering, where so many things were to be done, which ought to be done first. He was quickly called to action by the pilot, who, as he ran down the steps that led to the forecastle, exclaimed:

"Let every man take care of himself!"

When that man, who had been in nearly all the battles fought on the Mississippi River - who had run the batteries at

Vicksburg, and had twice, in the heat of action, swam from a sinking vessel - when *he* deserted his post, it was useless for any one to remain. The transport could be of no further use to them, and to stay on board was to court either death from the hot, blinding steam, or the shells that all the while came crashing into the boat, or capture and hard treatment at the hands of the rebels. So thought Frank, as he followed his men to the forecastle, intending to enter the cutter, and, if possible, run by the battery and reach the Mississippi.

The steam rolled over the lower deck in thick clouds, rendering it impossible for him to go aft. There was now but one way to reach the cutter, and that was to jump overboard and swim to her. This order was promptly given, and as promptly obeyed by the men, who sprang into the water, one after another, followed by Frank, who, however, had lingered a moment to pull off his side-arms and coat, which would only impede his progress, and to secure his dispatches, which he tied to his waist with a strong cord he happened to have in his pocket.

But when he reached the stern of the boat, he found that this means of escape had been destroyed. A shell from the battery had struck the cutter, and her wreck, still hold by the rope with which she had been made fast, floated along with the steamer, which was slowly drifting toward the bank. Only one of his men was to be seen, and that was the coxswain, who was holding on to the wreck, awaiting the appearance of his officer. The others, giving up all hopes of escape, had doubtless turned toward the shore.

"Now, here's a job, sir," said the coxswain, apparently as unconcerned as if there had not been a rebel within a hundred miles. "Here *is* a job. What's to be done now, sir?"

Frank had just asked himself the same question. He could easily reach the shore, which was but a few yards distant, but there he would certainly be captured by the rebels, who were running along the bank, yelling like demons.

There was but one course he could pursue and save himself and dispatches, and that was to swim down the river and endeavor to pass the battery. In the darkness he might escape undiscovered.

"Bob, are you a good swimmer?" he asked, turning to the coxswain.

"Yes sir! can swim all day," was the reply.

"Then follow me as silently as possible, and we may yet escape."

As Frank spoke, he swam down the river with swift, noiseless strokes, anxious to get as far as possible from the boat before the fire, which now began to make rapid headway, should light up the river and discover them to the rebels. The latter had ceased firing, and were scattered along the bank, making prisoners of the transport's crew as fast as they touched the shore. When Frank had reached the place where the battery was stationed, he turned upon his back, and allowed himself to float along with the current, and, aided by the darkness and the smoke of the burning transport, which blew down the river, he and his companion passed the dangerous point undiscovered. Here Frank again struck out, his every movement followed by the coxswain, who was close behind him, and who floated through the water like a cork.

For nearly an hour they remained in the river, and it was not until the shouts of the rebels could be no longer heard, that Frank, feeling for the present safe from pursuit, swam to the shore and sat down to rest, and to determine upon their future movements.

CHAPTER IX

UP THE WASHITA

All noise of pursuit, if any had been made, had died away, and not a sound disturbed the stillness of the woods. But Frank had learned, by experience, that silence was not indicative of safety, for it might, at any moment, be broken by the report of muskets, or a sudden demand for surrender from enemies who had followed them so silently that their approach had not been discovered. He bent suspicious glances upon the woods on all sides of him, and was ready to plunge into the water again upon hearing the least sounds of pursuit.

What had become of the wounded pilot, the lieutenant, and the rest of the cutter's crew? All who had succeeded in reaching the shore, were, beyond a doubt, prisoners.

Frank shuddered when he thought of the hard fare and harder treatment that awaited the poor fellows, recalling to mind incidents of his own capture and escape, which made him doubly anxious to reach the Mississippi as soon as possible, where he would be safe among friends.

After resting nearly an hour, for their long swim had wearied them, they continued their flight down the river, being careful to keep close to the bank, so that in case of emergency they could again take to the water. The shore was covered with logs and bushes, and their progress was slow and laborious. But daylight came at length, and shortly afterward they discovered a transport coming up the river. When she arrived opposite to them, Frank hailed her, and the boat landed and took them on board. Frank gave the information that there was a battery above, and the captain, not liking the idea of trusting his unarmed vessel within range of its guns, ordered the pilot to round-to and start down the river again. The order was obeyed at once, and Frank and the coxswain, who now began to breathe more freely, went below and stood before the fire-doors to dry their clothing. About noon they arrived at the Mississippi River, the transport landing alongside the vessel of the commanding naval officer, to whom Frank delivered his dispatches in triumph, at the same time apologizing for his appearance, for he was without coat, hat, or side-arms.

Among these dispatches of the admiral were orders for two tin-clads to report at Alexandria. These vessels were to be used to keep the banks clear of rebels, to carry dispatches, and to convoy unarmed steamers up and down the river. The necessary orders were promptly issued, and in a short time the tin-clads came alongside; their commanders received their instructions, after which the vessels steamed up Red River, one of them having Frank and the coxswain on board. The former had in his possession several official documents addressed to the admiral. If he could have seen the inside of one of them, he would have found (greatly to his surprise) that it contained a complete history of the run from Alexandria, that it spoke in the highest terms of his skill and bravery, and ended with a recommendation for a master's appointment. This letter had been written by the captain to whom Frank had delivered his dispatches, he having learned the full particulars from the coxswain, whom he had summoned into his presence while Frank was in the wardroom eating his dinner. The sailor described all that had happened in glowing language, dwelling with a good deal of emphasis upon the "pluck" displayed by his young officer, and the ignorance and cowardice of the lieutenant, and ended with saying, "He didn't think of nothing, sir, but them dispatches; and it an't every man that could have saved 'em, sir." The captain fully agreed with the coxswain, and when the latter was dismissed, he gave his pants a vigorous hitch, and said to himself, "If Mr. Nelson don't get another stripe around his arm now, may I be keelhauled." And one, to have seen him, would have thought that he was as much pleased at the prospect as though he was about to receive the appointment himself. Frank, of course, knew nothing of this, and little imagining that he was carrying a recommendation for his promotion, he put the letters carefully away in his pocket, thinking, no doubt, they were all-important official documents.

A short time before dark they arrived at the junction of the Black and Washita Rivers, where Frank found the Michigan anchored, in company with four or five other gun-boats. He reported his safe return to his captain, and then went into the wardroom and sat down to report to the admiral by letter, according to his instructions. After all he had passed through, one would suppose that his report would have been a long one; but he wisely thought that all the admiral cared to know was that his dispatches had been safely delivered. He therefore wrote, in the briefest manner -

"I have the honor to report that, in obedience to your orders of the 20th inst., I took passage on board the United States army transport "Key-West," for the mouth of Red River, with dispatches, which were delivered into the hands of the commanding naval officer there. I have to-day returned on board my vessel."

This was all. No glowing description of the gallant manner in which he had taken the transport by the battery, no mention of the ever-watchful eye he had kept upon his dispatches, or of his long swim from the burning wreck, but a few simple lines, that told the admiral all he wished to know; namely, that his letters had reached their destination. This report Frank placed before the captain, who wrote upon it "approved and respectfully forwarded," (for all letters from subordinate officers to the admiral had to pass through the captain's hands,) and the letter was put into the general mail. Frank then, in obedience to the captain's order, proceeded to give that gentleman a minute account of the manner in which he had executed his orders, together with the names of the men belonging to the cutter's crew who were missing, and wound up with the request that "something might be done for the coxswain," for he was a brave man, and a good sailor. As the Michigan had but one boatswain's mate, (she was entitled to two,) the captain determined to promote the man, who was at once summoned into the cabin and presented with the boatswain's whistle. He retired, proud of his promotion, and firm in his belief that "the captain and Mr. Nelson were the best men afloat."

Frank, so weary that he could scarcely walk, was glad to get to bed; but the captain sat for a long time at his desk, writing a letter to the admiral, which contained the statement that, in his opinion, "Acting Ensign Frank Nelson, by the gallant manner in which he had executed the important business intrusted to him, had nobly earned his promotion, and, by the skill and judgment he had exhibited in handling the transport, had shown that he was fully capable of taking charge of a *vessel of his own*, and that his past history, taken in connection with his recent exploit, was sufficient guarantee that the honor of the flag would never suffer in his hands."

Frank, all unconscious of the admiration his gallant behavior had excited in the mind of the captain, slept soundly until daylight, when he was called up to get the vessel under way. The expedition was composed of five gun-boats, and its destination was Monroe, a small town about two hundred miles up Washita River. Its object was to capture cotton, and to destroy any fortifications that might be found along the banks. The remainder of the fleet, which was at Alexandria when Frank left, had gone up Red River, toward Shreveport. Had he been allowed his choice in the matter, Frank would have preferred to accompany the latter expedition, as he then would have been able, after Shreveport had been captured, to visit the prison in which he had been confined, and from which he had escaped in so remarkable a manner. He thought over all the scenes through which he had passed - his capture, the march to Shreveport, his flight from the prison, the bayonet-fight in the woods, the chase by blood-hounds - and they seemed to him like a dream.

George Le Dell, who was the officer of the deck, stood close beside Frank, gazing about as if every object that met his eye was a familiar one. Every turn of the paddle-wheels was bringing him nearer to the home of his childhood, from which he was now excluded by the stern mandate of his rebel father. Ever since he had been attached to the Michigan, he and Frank had been bosom friends. The dangers through which they had passed while fugitives from a rebel prison - their hair-breadth escapes from recapture - could never be forgotten. No one on board besides Frank knew any thing of George's past history. In accordance with the latter's desire, the secret was closely kept, and no one imagined that the pale, quiet young officer was any relation to the rebel general whose house it had been ordered should be burned. Ever since the receipt of that order, every one remarked that George Le Dell had been unusually thoughtful, but no one knew the cause.

"Mr. Nelson," said he, at length, "I wish I could have gone up Red River. I want to see home once more, but I don't want to stand by and see the old house burned over the heads of my mother and sisters. I don't deny that the order is a just one, but I don't want to see it executed. I begin to believe that I am a good prophet," he continued, after a moment's pause. "I told father, in the last letter I ever wrote to him, that this war would bring him nothing but suffering and disgrace, and I think he will find that I told the truth."

As George ceased speaking, he turned and walked to another part of the deck, to meet the captain, who at that moment came out of his cabin.

Among all the ship's company, there was but one that could sympathize with George, and that one was Frank. The young officer cherished an honest enmity toward the traitors whose bloody hands were stretched out to pull down the Old Flag under which his ancestors had fought and died, but when Frank looked upon the pale face of his messmate, and listened to his oft-repeated sentiments of loyalty, and heard him, in his quiet way, expressing his firm belief in the final triumph of the Government and the total overthrow of the rebellion, and when he witnessed his quiet submission to his cruel fate, knowing that he was cut off from all further intercourse with his relatives, he could not help pitying both him and his rebel parents. But he knew, from those letters he had read, and which George still preserved, and from what he had witnessed on that memorable night when he and his companions had stopped at the plantation and asked for food, that the general and his family had taken part with the rebellion, not to secure any rights which they imagined had been denied them, but to assist in "establishing a confederacy of their own, whose corner-stone should be slavery," and to destroy "every vestige of the old Union." Like George, he knew that the order to burn the house was a just one; but he would have been much better pleased had some other boat been selected to execute it. He did not pity the rebels so much, but he did not want to witness the sorrow his messmate would experience when he saw the home of his boyhood enveloped in flames.

The next day, as the two friends stood together on deck, George suddenly said -

"We're almost there. I know these woods well. I've caught many a string of fish off that log that lies in the water just ahead."

About half a mile further on, the Michigan came round a sharp bend in the river, and they saw the plantation before them. Every thing looked just as it did on that long-to-be-remembered night when George had suddenly presented himself before his relatives, who thought him safe in the prison at Tyler. There were the broad stone steps that led up to the portico on which the major had stood while making known his wants, and just in front of them were the posts to which the general and his sons had fastened their horses before entering the house.

The fleet did not stop, as they had expected, but kept on up the river, and in a few moments more the plantation was out of sight. No doubt the burning of the house was to be put off until their return.

The expedition reached Monroe without mishap, and without seeing a single armed rebel, only stopping now and then to pick up cotton, which was scattered all along the bank. The vessels remained at anchor in front of the town for two days, and after burning the public buildings, and picking up some escaped Union prisoners, started down the river again. The Michigan led the way, and on the afternoon of the second day came to anchor in front of General Le Dell's plantation.

"Mr. Nelson," said the captain, as he stepped down out of the pilot-house, "order two companies of small-armed men to be called away, and you and Mr. Le Dell get ready to go on shore with me. By the way," he added, turning to George, "I have orders to burn out this rebel namesake of yours."

"So I have heard, sir," replied George, while not a muscle of his face quivered to show the surprise and sorrow he felt at being obliged to accompany the expedition ashore. He had hoped that some other officer would be chosen to accompany the captain, but he could not ask to be excused from duty without exciting suspicions. The reason why he did not wish to go could be easily guessed, and if the truth became known, it would be followed by what he particularly desired to avoid - the sympathy of all his messmates. He would accompany the expedition, but he would neither enter the house or go into the presence of his mother and sisters, and he might return without being recognized. By the time he had buckled on his sword and returned to the deck the men were ready, when, in obedience to Frank's order, he marched them on board the tug, which lay at the stern of the Michigan. When they reached the shore, Frank instructed George to post sentries all around the house, both to guard against surprise, and also to prevent the escape of any rebel soldiers who might chance to be in the building, after which he accompanied the captain to the door, where they were met by Mrs. Le Dell and her daughters, who coldly received their salutations, and waited for them to make known the object of their visit.

"Madam," said the captain, addressing himself to Mrs. Le Dell, "I am ordered to burn your house."

"I have been expecting it for a long time," was the reply.

"I will give you a reasonable time," continued the captain, "to remove your valuables."

The lady then requested that an hour might be allowed her to send for a neighbor, who lived several miles distant, to come with his team to remove the furniture to a place of safety, as all the wagons about the plantation had been given up to the rebel army. This was granted, and a note, which was first presented for the inspection of the captain, was at once dispatched to summon the neighbor.

In the meantime, Frank and George were strolling about the plantation, the latter feasting his eyes on every familiar object, and recalling to mind incidents of the "good old times," as he expressed it. Frank also recognized two objects; one was the barn where he and his fellow-fugitives had halted to hold a consultation before going up to the house; and the other was the fence behind which the captain had left their prisoner, bound hand and foot. While thus engaged, a little boy, who had approached them without being discovered, suddenly called out,

"George!"

The latter turned, as the familiar voice reached his ear, and held out his hands to his brother, who sprang toward him, threw his arms around his neck, and burst into tears. There was one among George's relatives who still remembered and loved him.

"George," sobbed the little fellow, "are you a Yankee 'bolitionist?"

Tears choked George's utterance, and the boy, suddenly breaking from his arms, ran toward the house, and scrambling up the steps, burst into the room where the captain and ladies were seated, and astonished them all with:

"Mother, mother! George is here! He's come back!"

Both mother and daughter appeared to be considerably agitated upon receiving this news, and the captain noticing it, the suspicion flashed across his mind that it was one of their rebel friends. He glanced out at the door, and saw his two officers standing quietly together, the sentinels walking their beats, and felt satisfied that the rebel, whoever he was, might consider himself a prisoner.

"Who do you mean, my little man?" he asked, putting his hand on the boy's head. "What is his other name?"

"George Le Dell," replied the boy, promptly. "He's my brother. He's out there," and he pointed toward the place where George and Frank were standing.

"Is that your brother?" asked the captain in surprise, as he turned toward Mrs. Le Dell for an explanation.

"I have a son in the Federal navy," replied the lady.

"Then, madam," said the captain, "if that young man out there is your son, allow me to say that you have every reason to be proud of him."

At this moment the neighbor for whom they had sent arrived, and he and the captain held a long conversation; after which, to his surprise, Frank was ordered to collect the men and march them on board the tug. The Michigan remained at her anchorage until the flag-ship of the expedition came down, when the two captains had a short consultation, and both vessels got under way and steamed down the river. The reason given why the order to burn the house was not executed was this: Unlike the majority of rebel commanders, General Le Dell had always treated Union prisoners who had fallen into his hands with the greatest humanity. Although he seemed to be particularly spiteful toward George, whom he called a "young traitor," he always endeavored to make the condition of other prisoners as tolerable as possible. The truth of this was attested by the soldiers they had picked up at Monroe, all of whom were officers, and they had done much toward saving the property. The captain of the Michigan had delayed to fulfill his orders until the arrival of his superior, in order to communicate some news he had received from the man who had been sent to remove the furniture, and when the flag-ship arrived, the order had been countermanded.

"Perhaps every thing will come out right after the war," said George, as the two friends stood watching the plantation as long as it remained in eight. "If it does, we'll have the old house to live in."

On the way down the river, large quantities of cotton were captured, which made both officers and men look forward to a good share of prize-money, and one afternoon - about a week after leaving Monroe - they reached Black River in safety.

CHAPTER X

THE PROMOTION

The next day, in obedience to orders from the admiral, the Michigan steamed up Red River, and came to an anchor in front of Fort De Russy. A few rebel soldiers had taken possession of the fortifications, and the vessel had scarcely dropped her anchor when they opened upon her with muskets. All hands were ordered under cover, and for two days were kept closely confined below. The bullets, which constantly whistled over the deck, did no damage beyond cutting down the flag - which, however was promptly hoisted again - and battering up the officers' rooms on the quarter-deck, which were not iron-clad. Several attempts were made to dislodge the rebels, but, as usual, without success. On the third day, however, a heavy firing up the river, in the direction of Alexandria, announced that the expedition was returning, and the rebels, fearing capture, hastily withdrew. Toward evening the fleet came in sight, some of the transports having gun-boats alongside of them for protection. The entire fleet bore marks of the handiwork of the rebels, in the shape of battered casemates, broken chimneys, and shattered upper works. Little had been accomplished beyond the capture of cotton, and both officers and men teemed delighted to find themselves once more on the way to the Mississippi River.

In about an hour after the first boats of the fleet had made their appearance, a tin-clad came down, bearing the admiral's flag, and rounded-to and landed a short distance below the

Michigan. Close behind her came another of the mosquito fleet, towed by a transport. Both vessels were badly cut up, especially the gun-boat, which was almost a wreck. Both chimneys had either been broken off by branches of trees or shattered by a shell, and her casemates were pierced in a hundred places. Her engines had also been disabled, and her wheel hung motionless in the water. Still she retained enough of her former appearance for Frank to recognize in her his old vessel, the Boxer; besides, he saw his cousin on the guards waving his handkerchief to him. While Frank stood watching the vessel, wondering how any of her crew could have escaped, and how Archie had conducted himself during the fights through which he had passed, the captain came up out of his cabin and exclaimed:

"Mr. Nelson, you're wanted on board the flagship! Don't wait to get your side-arms, but go at once. The admiral is in a great hurry to see you!"

Frank, wondering what new orders he was about to receive, ran down the ladder that led to the afterguard, reached the shore on a plank that extended from the stern of the vessel to the bank, and in a short time was in the presence of the admiral.

That gentleman was so busy that he did not notice Frank, until one of his clerks exclaimed:

"Admiral! here's Captain Nelson, sir."

"Ah, yes," said the admiral, scarcely looking up from his work. "Sit down, captain; I'm very busy just at present."

Captain! Frank knew that neither the admiral nor his clerks were in the habit of making mistakes, but he thought they were certainly mistaken this time. Perhaps they were so busy they had not taken time to see who he was. But he was not kept long in suspense, for the admiral, after signing his name to several documents, turned in his chair, and picking up some letters that lay on his desk, handed them to Frank, saying:

"Captain, there are your orders. I only wanted to see you to say that I wish them obeyed with the least possible delay. Have the Boxer back here as soon as you can, for I want to use her. Get your baggage on board and start at once."

Frank, so bewildered that he scarcely knew what the admiral was saying, took the letters and hurried back to the Michigan. The captain met him at the gangway, and extending his hand, said, with a smile:

"I'm sorry to have you leave us, Mr. Nelson. I suppose you have got it?"

"I have something, sir," replied Frank, "but I don't know what it is."

As he spoke, he tore open one of the envelopes, and hastily running his eye over the letter it contained, found, to his astonishment, that he was an acting master. The next one he opened was an order for him to report "to the commanding fficer of the U. S. S. Boxer for duty and *command of that vessel*." The other contained instructions for him to "proceed to Cairo without delay, and place his vessel under repairs, and as soon as she was put in condition for service, to return and report to the admiral."

"Just as I expected," said the captain, who seemed to be as highly elated as Frank himself. "Just as I expected, sir. You deserve it, and I congratulate you."

Frank made some reply, in his excitement he hardly knew what, and hurried off to pack his trunk and bed-clothes. This being accomplished, his baggage was carried to the cutter, which lay alongside, and after taking leave of the captain and his messmates, he stepped into the boat and started for his vessel, which still lay at the bank, below the flagship, with the transport which was to tow her to Cairo. As he stepped on board the Boxer, he was met by Archie, and several of his old messmates, who greeted him cordially. The executive officer was in command, and to him Frank showed his orders, and requested that his baggage might be conveyed into the cabin. He then went on deck, and after ascertaining that the transport was ready to start, ordered the line cast off, and both vessels were soon on their course down the river.

After finding they were fairly under way, Frank, accompanied by Archie, went into the cabin, and sat down to collect his thoughts, for, in the excitement of his unexpected promotion, he moved like one in a dream. The cabin steward had already taken his trunk into his state-room, and was engaged in making his bed. Captain Nelson! How strangely it sounded; and Frank repeated it several times, and gazed about the cabin as if he could scarcely believe that he was awake. He read his appointment and orders over and over again, both to fully understand what was required of him, and to convince himself that he was in reality the commander of a vessel. When he was made the executive officer of the very boat he now commanded, he had reached the height of his ambition, and his present position was a step higher than he had dared to look.

The captain of a gun-boat generally lives in a little world of his own. He has a cabin all to himself, messes alone, and rarely has intercourse with his officers, except upon business. If he has a messmate, it is either a clerk, or the paymaster or doctor of the vessel. Frank was not entitled to a clerk, but he had a paymaster, and, at his request, Archie at once commenced the removal of his baggage into one of the vacant state-rooms in the cabin. While thus engaged, the orderly announced the executive officer, who entered to inquire if Frank had any orders to give. The latter replied that he had not, and for nearly an hour he remained in conversation with the executive, during which he learned the exact state of affairs about decks. Every thing appeared to be going on smoothly, and Frank had no desire to show his authority by issuing unnecessary orders. One by one the wardroom and steerage officers came in to congratulate the young commander, and when bed-time came they returned to their quarters, saying among themselves that "Captain Nelson didn't feel any bigger in his new position than he would if he were nothing but a Johnny master's mate."

One afternoon, after they had reached the Mississippi River, as Frank sat at his desk, writing a letter to his mother, and Archie lay on the sofa close by, engaged in reading, there was a commotion on deck, and the orderly burst into the cabin, exclaiming -

"Rebels, cap'n! A battery just ahead, sir!" And he had scarcely spoken, when there was a roar of cannon, and the shells burst over and about the vessels.

"Call to quarters," said Frank, as he sprang to his feet and ran into his room after his side-arms and the keys to the magazine.

The orderly disappeared, followed by Archie, who, throwing his book into the furthest corner of the cabin, ran on deck, without even waiting to get his hat.

After ordering the executive, who met him at the door, to have the lamps in the magazine lighted, and to prepare for action, Frank ran into the pilothouse, and looking up the river, discovered a smoke arising from a point half a mile in advance of them.

"Captain," shouted the commander of the transport, who stood in his pilot-house, "what do you want me to do?"

"Take us up the river as fast as you can," shouted Frank, in reply.

The captain had evidently seen some stirring times while up Red River. He was not accustomed to the noise and confusion of battle, and his actions indicated that he did not like the idea of attempting to run by the battery. But his orders from the admiral were to take the Boxer to Cairo as soon as possible, and he dared not disobey them.

"All ready below, sir," was the word at this moment passed up through the trumpet.

All the guns on board the Boxer were pointed at the battery, and the crew impatiently waited for the order to fire. Frank stood at his post, watching the battery through a spy-glass, and waiting until they should come to close quarters, so that he could make every shot count. All this while the shells had been dropping into the water, and shrieking through the air about the vessels, and one or two had found a lodgement in the wheel-house of the transport. They kept on in silence until they arrived almost opposite the battery, which stood out in plain view, unprotected by levee or other breastwork, and Frank then gave the order to open upon them. The crash that followed the order, as every gun that could be brought to bear upon the battery belched forth its contents, was terrific. Shells and canister rattled over the bank, cutting down the rebel gunners, and disabling one of their cannon. As quickly as possible, the guns were reloaded, and almost before the rebels had recovered from their panic, another broadside was poured into them, and when the smoke cleared away, the battery was standing deserted. Here was an opportunity that, to Frank, had he possessed men enough to back him up, would not have been lost; he would have landed, and captured the battery. But he was ignorant of the force of the rebels. There might be a regiment of them hidden away in the woods - enough to have captured the vessels the moment they touched the bank - and to have lost the Boxer scarcely a week after he had been placed in command of her would have been a misfortune indeed. He kept on up the river, shelling the woods as long as he could bring a gun to bear upon them.

In a few days they arrived at Cairo, where Frank reported to the commandant of the station, and his vessel was at once placed in the hands of the workmen at the navy-yard. The work was rapidly pushed forward, and at the end of a month she was declared ready for service, and after she had been furnished with a full crew from the receiving ship, and Archie had laid in a stock of paymaster's stores, the Boxer, in obedience to orders, started down the river to report to the admiral.

CHAPTER XI

THE RIVAL SPIES

They found the admiral at Natchez, and when Frank had reported his arrival, he was ordered to take his station at Gaines' Landing - a place noted for guerrillas - which they reached in safety. For two or three days, nothing worthy of note transpired, the rebels, if there were any about, being careful not to show themselves.

One night, while Frank was walking the deck, arm-in-arm with his cousin, the officer on watch approached, and said, in a low voice:

"Look there, sir! What kind of a craft is that?"

Frank looked in the direction indicated, and an object about the size of a man's head could be dimly seen in the water, silently but rapidly approaching the vessel. It came from toward the nearest shore, and the thought that it was a torpedo instantly flushed through his mind. Taking the spy-glass from the quarter-master, he leveled it at the object, and could distinctly see that it was a human head, and that it belonged to some one who was an excellent swimmer, for he was making rapid progress through the water.

"I don't see any torpedo there," said he, at length, handing the glass to his cousin, "for the fellow, whoever he is, is using both hands." Then raising his it voice, he called out, "Who comes there?"

"A friend," was the scarcely audible reply.

"Come on board here."

"That's just what I want to do," answered the man, who, with a few more strokes, was near enough to be seized by the quarter-master - who had ran below with a lantern - and lifted upon the guards.

"Who are you, and what are you doing here at this time of night?" asked Frank, as soon as the man had come on deck.

"My name is William Striker," was the answer, "and I am an escaped Union scout."

Frank took the lantern from the quarter-master's hand and held it up, so that he could obtain a good view of the man's face. He was certain he had seen it before, but could not remember where.

"I have a better memory than you, sir," said the man at length. "I have seen you before. I met you in the trenches at Vicksburg."

As the man spoke, he produced a bundle of wet papers, from which he selected one that he handed to Frank. It was the appointment of major, and addressed to William Striker, United States Scout. But this was no proof that the man was in reality what he professed to be, for Frank remembered that he had once passed himself off as Lieutenant Somers, of the rebel army, and had shown his appointment and orders to prove it. It was true that he wore the dress of a Union major, but that might have been obtained in the same manner that Frank once got his rebel uniform. There was something suspicious in a man's presenting himself on board the vessel at that time of night, and in so uncommon a manner.

"Well," said Frank, "if you were in the trenches at Vicksburg, tell me something that happened there."

The soldier then told Frank of the experiment of which the latter had made use to see "how far off the rebels were," during which he lost his cap, the rebel who captured it offering to "trade" for it a tattered slouch-hat with a bullet-hole in it, and informed him that he was the scout who had told him the story of his "partner" Sam, and their raid into the rebel camp, which resulted in the capture of Colonel Peckham. He also related other little incidents which Frank had not forgotten, and which proved that he was in reality the scout whom he had met in the trenches, and not a rebel spy, as he had at first feared. Being fully satisfied on this point, the major was conducted into the cabin, and while he was exchanging his wet clothes for some that Frank and Archie had provided for him, the former ordered his steward to prepare supper for their guest, for he knew, by experience, that a man who had been a prisoner among the rebels was hungry. The major sat down to the table with a most ravenous appetite, and the good things the steward had prepared rapidly disappeared. When he had finished his meal, in answer to Frank's inquiry how he came to be a prisoner, he gave the following account of his adventures, which he remarked were a "little ahead of any thing he had ever gone through."

"In the first place," said he, "I must tell you what became of my comrade, Sam, as it was in endeavoring to assist him that I was captured. His career as a scout, although an exciting one, full of stirring adventures and hair-breadth escapes, was brought to a close soon after the capture of Vicksburg.

"When the army again took up its line of march, we made several excursions into the rebel lines, and one night we stopped at a plantation-house to shelter ourselves from the rain, for it was storming violently, and also to see if we could not pick up some information that might be of use to us. The only inmate of the house was an old woman, who, believing us to be rebels, talked freely with us on all subjects; and during the conversation, which finally turned upon scouting, informed us that there was a scout in the rebel army who was far ahead of any "Yank" that ever lived. He was described as a daring, quick-witted fellow, and many a disaster that had befallen us was owing to him. As I listened to the stories told of him, I came to the conclusion that there was a good deal of truth in them, and that some spy must indeed have been in our camp, for the woman was acquainted with several moves we had made, and which had been defeated, the particulars of which, I thought, were known only to the general and his staff. This led me to believe that the scout, whoever he was, staid about head-quarters, else how could he obtain so much information.

"The woman seemed to be well acquainted with him and his movements, and told us of several of his exploits, which, if true, showed the spy to be a man admirably fitted for his position. I listened attentively to all she said, in hopes I should learn something of his personal appearance, for I had made up my mind that as soon as I could find out his movements, he and I would have a meeting, But all I could learn was that his name was Bob Cole.

"'Well,' said I,'do you know that as long as I have been in the army, I have never seen this man?'"

"'Haven't yer!' exclaimed the woman, in surprise. 'Wal, come to think, I don't know as that is so funny, arter all, 'cause he's in the Yankee camp most of the time, an', as they think he is one of them, he goes an' comes when he pleases, He's a smart one, I tell yer. Some of the boys told me that he is a goin' to bring in a prisoner this week, in the shape of a Yankee scout an' spy. Bill Striker is his name, I believe. Do yer know him?'

"I couldn't help starting when I found that I was known to this noted rebel; but the woman didn't notice it, and I replied:

"Oh, yes! I've heard of him.'

"'Cordin' to all accounts,' continued the woman, 'this Yankee an't much behind Bob, for he has often been in our camp, an' he don't allers go back empty-handed. If he ketches a feller in an out-of-the-way place, he is sartin to gobble him up. But his time is most up now, 'kase Bob never fails in any thing when he onct gets his mind sot on it, an' when I heerd that he was a goin' to ketch this Yank, I believed he would do it.

"It was very encouraging to sit there and listen to a person talk so confidently of my speedy capture; but, as it happened, I had been put on my guard, and another thing, I didn't have quite as much faith in Bob Cole as his rebel friends had, and was in no way concerned about his being able to fulfill his promise. It set me to thinking, however, and I determined I would not sleep sound until I had found him, and then there would be a prisoner taken, sure; but it wouldn't be Bill Striker.

"'What kind of a looking man is he?' I asked, at length.

"'Oh, he's a' -

"Just at this moment we heard several horsemen going by the house, and Sam exclaimed:

"'There are some of our boys now. Perhaps we are wanted.'

"I knew well enough what he meant. Although we had frequently met rebels while scouting about through their lines, we were not at all fond of them, and did not want to be in their company if we could help it.

"Those who had just gone by might at any moment return and enter the house; and besides, it occurred to me that if I was so well known to the rebel spy, I was not safe except in our own camp. I might, at any time, run into a trap he had laid for me. At any rate, we thought it best to get within our lines as soon as possible; so, without waiting to hear the woman's description of Bob Cole, we bid her good night.

"We reached our camp in safety, reported our return, and the next morning I walked up to headquarters, where I remained until dark, talking with the general's hostler, and keeping an ear open for news, but was obliged to go away without hearing any. The next day I was kept busy carrying dispatches, and when I returned at night, I learned that Sam had gone into the rebel camp, as they were making some movement, the particulars of which the general was anxious to learn. I thought nothing of it at the time, but when night came and he did not return, I began to fear that he had been captured or killed. It then occurred to me that if I could get back to the house where lived the woman who had told us of Bob Cole, I might learn something that would be to my advantage; so I put on my rebel uniform, and in a few moments was out of the lines. I reached the house in safety, and was delighted to find there were no rebels about. The woman seemed glad to see me, brought me a cup of water to drink, and after a few minutes' conversation exclaimed:

"'Wal, they've gobbled up one of them fellers!'

"'Which one?' I asked.

"'I don't know his name. Bob done it. He seed him leave the Yankee camp, an' follered him, an' while they were ridin' along together, he tuk out his pistol an' told the Yank to give up his we'pons; but the feller wouldn't do it, an' Bob had to shoot him. But he didn't kill him; he only shot him through the shoulder. He's sartin to be hung.'

"You can easily imagine my feelings as I sat there and listened to this. It required a strong effort to subdue my feelings.

"'How does Bob Cole disguise himself?' I asked, in as firm a voice as I could command. 'What does he do in the Yankee camp?'

"'That's what nobody, 'sides Bob an' the general, knows,' answered the woman. 'Didn't you never see him? He's a little man, has black hair and eyes, wears no whiskers, and allers rides a little gray horse. He's smart, I tell yer.'

"After talking awhile longer with the woman without learning any thing further, I mounted my horse and returned to camp. While I was eating my supper, I called to mind all the scouts with whom I was acquainted, but not one of them answered to the description of Bob Cole. There was one man in camp, however, who *did* answer the description, and that was the general's hostler. Could it he possible that he was the spy?

"At this moment an orderly entered to tell me that I was wanted at head-quarters. I followed him to the general's tent, received my orders, and began to get ready for the journey. As I came out of the tent I met the hostler, who inquired:

"'Are you off again to-night, Bill?'

"I replied in the affirmative, and he continued:

"'Well, good luck to you. Don't let the rebs get hold of you.'

"I mounted my horse and rode out of the camp, fully satisfied that if he was the spy I would soon know it.

"The night was very dark, but I had traveled the road often enough to be well acquainted with it, and in an hour after I left our camp, I had passed the rebel sentries, and was fairly within their lines. As I was riding quietly along, keeping a good look-out on all sides, and pausing now and then to listen, I suddenly heard the clatter of horses' hoofs behind me, and some one called out, in a low voice:

"Bill! Bill Striker!'

"I instantly stopped, and a moment afterward up galloped the hostler.

"'Don't make so much noise, Jim,' said I, nastily. 'But what on earth brings you here? Where are you going?'

"'I'm after you,' he replied. 'The general told me to overtake you, and say that he had neglected to give you some very important orders.'

"All this while he had been coming nearer and nearer to me, and having now got within reach, he suddenly seized my bridle, and presenting a revolver, exclaimed:

"'Bill Striker, your scouting is up now! You're my prisoner!'

"If he imagined that he had taken me by surprise he was very much mistaken. In an instant I had knocked aside the revolver, which exploded, sending the ball harmlessly past my head, and in a moment more I had wrested the weapon from him. Then, almost before he had time to think twice, I lifted him off his horse and laid him across my saddle, in front of me, as if he had been a bag of corn. He was very strong, as wiry as an eel, and struggled most desperately; but I had him at disadvantage, and when I thought of Sam, who was now a prisoner through the treachery of this fellow, I felt as if I had the strength of ten men. By the time I had fairly got hold of him, I was tearing down the road toward our lines, while his own horse had gone on toward the rebel camp. My only danger was in being cut off by the pickets. These passed, I would be safe, for I had no fears of being overtaken. There was no time to avoid them in jumping over fences and running through fields, for I knew that the report of the revolver had been heard, and that, unless I could reach our lines in a very few moments, Bob Cole would again be a free man and I would be the prisoner. I used my spurs freely, and my horse, which seemed to understand that he was called upon to make use of his best speed, carried us over the ground at a tremendous rate. In a short time I came within sight of a fire burning by the side of the road. I heard a loud command to halt, followed by the noise of a bullet as it whistled by my head, and the pickets were passed in safety. Half an hour afterward I dismounted in front of the general's tent, and delivered up my prisoner. You can't imagine how surprised our boys were to learn that we had had a rebel spy in our camp so long without knowing it. Bob Cole had played his cards remarkably well, and if Sam and I had not stopped at that house to get out of the rain, there's no knowing how much longer he would have been at liberty. But he was safe in the guard-house at last, and I must confess that I breathed more freely. If he was the only rebel who knew me, there was now no danger of running into a trap laid for my capture. My first hard work must be to attempt Sam's release. I knew it would be worse than useless to return to the rebel camp that night, for it had been aroused, and my own chances of escape would be none of the surest; so I let two days pass before setting out, and then I did not follow my usual course, but took a roundabout way to get behind their camp, where I would not run so much risk of meeting the pickets.

"I reached the lines in safety, and as I was riding along by the side of the road, keeping my horse on the grass, to make as little noise as possible, I heard horsemen approaching, and presently up galloped a party of rebels. I thought they would pass without discovering me, but was mistaken, for one of them drew in his horse and exclaimed -

"'Wal, ef here an't another,' and I was speedily surrounded, and commanded to 'hand over my we'pons.'

"'Look here, boys,' said I, 'I've got a pass,' and I made a motion to produce it.

"'Oh, we don't want to see your pass,' said the corporal who had charge of the squad; 'we've seed a dozen to-night that wasn't no 'count. You must go to the guard-house, 'cause you know it's the general's orders that nobody goes out o' camp.'

"This showed me that I was not suspected of being a Federal, but was arrested as one of their own men who was endeavoring to get out of the lines.

"'I know it's mighty hard,' continued the corporal, 'not to let a feller go home, when p'rhaps it an't five miles off; but orders is orders, you know. Howsomever, you wont hev no trouble to get out o' the guard-house, 'cause - by gum! ef here an't some more,' and, as he spoke, he left me, and rode up to three men who were crouching in the fence-corner by the roadside. These were speedily secured, and we went on our way toward the guard-house. The rebel army, it appeared, was encamped in a part of the country where a number of regiments had been raised, and the men, anxious to see home and friends once more, were deserting by hundreds - 'taking French,' as we call it. As we rode along, I learned something, from the conversation of my captors, that made me wish I had never taken Bob Cole prisoner, and that was, that Sam had died from the effects of the wound he had received while resisting the rebel. This was, perhaps, better than being hung, but how I wished I had known it before taking the spy to camp. I had put myself in danger without being able to be of any assistance to Sam, and I now set my wits to work to conjure up some plan for escape.

"Finally, after capturing one more rebel who was about to 'take French,' we reached the guard house, which was a rickety old barn. As we entered the door, the rebels, with whom the house was filled, greeted us with loud yells, and slapped us on our backs, as though they looked upon our capture as a most excellent joke. The majority of our fellow-prisoners were confined for attempting to leave the camp to visit their friends; but putting them in the guard-house was only a farce, for I had not been in the room fifteen minutes before I saw three men make their escape through a window. I determined to try the same thing; so, after waiting a few moments, to see that they were not brought back, I walked up to the window and looked out. A sentinel was standing at the corner of the building, but as soon as he saw me he shouldered his gun and walked off, whistling. It was plain that he had no objections to my making my escape if I wished to do so, and, as soon as he was out of sight, I crawled out of the window, dropped to the ground, and walked off with an appearance of unconcern I was very far from feeling.

"I had lost my horse, but that did not trouble me, for the camp was not far off, and I had no fears of pursuit. I had scarcely got safely out of their lines, however, before I became aware that I was followed. I turned and saw a party of men, who, keeping their horses on the grass at the side of the road, had succeeded in getting within pistol-shot before I heard them. As I sprang over a fence I heard my name pronounced, followed by the report of several revolvers and carbines, that sent the bullets about me altogether too close for comfort.

"Well, to make a long story short, I laid about in the woods for a month, making a raid now and then on a chicken-roost, to supply my commissary department; but all this while the rebels followed me like blood-hounds. I had gone miles out of my way - in fact, I did not know where I was, until one day I was in with a party of guerrillas. I told them I was a reb on French leave, and on my way to visit my friends, who lived on the opposite side of the river. From them I learned that the Mississippi was sixty miles distant, and was also informed that there was a gun-boat at Gaines's Landing, and was advised to keep out of her way. This was the best news I had heard in a long time, and I determined to make the best of my way here. I came off to the vessel in the night, because I did not know but there might be rebels on the watch, and as I was entirely unarmed, I did not want to run any risks. Since leaving our camp, I have traveled nearly two hundred miles without a weapon of any kind, not even a pocket-knife; and if either of you has ever been a prisoner, you can easily imagine that I am overjoyed to find myself safe among friends once more. And now, captain," continued the scout, "I have a proposition to make you. The leader of these guerrillas whom I met back in the country makes his head-quarters in a deserted plantation-house about forty miles from the river. He never has more than two or three men with him, the others being scattered over the country, stealing horses from both rebels and Union people. Now, I would like to help capture him and break up his band of guerrillas, for he's a perfect demon, and never takes any prisoners. There is a house about ten miles from here where we can get all the horses we need, and three or four men could do the job nicely. This guerrilla's brother was formerly the captain of the band, but he was killed by a party of rebels, just as he was about to hang a couple of Union prisoners he had taken - gun-boat men, I believe. His name is Thorne, and - what's the matter, captain?"

Frank had started upon hearing the name of the guerrilla chief at whose hands he and the mate had so nearly suffered death, and from which they were rescued by the Wild-cats, and just as he finished relating the story of the "Close Shave," the orderly entered the cabin and announced the dispatch-boat "General Lyon" approaching.

CHAPTER XII

A SCOUTING PARTY

Frank, of course, could not agree to the scout's proposition without first obtaining permission of either the admiral or Captain Wilson - the commander of the division to which the Boxer belonged. He did not know where to go to find the former, and besides, the latter had given him strict orders not to leave his station until relieved by some other vessel, and to allow no one to go ashore. The very nature of these orders put it out of his power to obtain liberty to carry out the proposed expedition. He went to bed pondering upon what the major had told him, and fell asleep without being able to conjure up any plan by which the capture of the rebel might be effected.

The next morning, while at breakfast, the orderly entered the cabin and reported a gun-boat approaching. Frank at once went on deck, and when he had made out her signals, he found, to his delight, that it was the Manhattan, the flagship of the division to which the Boxer belonged. After ordering the officer of the deck to have the gig called away, Frank ran into the cabin, put on his side-arms, and, in company with the major, put off to the iron-clad.

Captain Wilson received them cordially, listened with a good deal of interest to the scout's plan for the capture of the guerrilla, and finally gave Frank permission to "do as he pleased in the matter," adding, "You have never yet failed in an undertaking of this kind, and I shall fully expect you to succeed in the present instance. I will be here again in about a week, and you can turn the prisoner over to me." The confident manner in which the captain spoke of his success, made Frank more determined than ever to capture the guerrilla, if within the bounds of possibility. After giving a short report of the state of affairs on his station, he returned to the Boxer, highly delighted with the result of the interview. Archie was no less pleased, for, although he had not said a word about accompanying his cousin, he looked upon it as a settled thing that he was to be one of the expedition. Frank, who knew the danger of the undertaking, and was anxious to keep Archie out of harm's way, would have preferred to leave him behind; but, as the latter had shown, in a remarkable manner, that he was equal to any emergency, the young commander could not deny him on the ground that he had never "smelt powder."

The major advised Frank to take at least one more man; and this one was soon forthcoming in the shape of Tom, the coxswain of the first cutter, the same who had been left in charge of the boat on the night that Frank and Archie had broken up the head-quarters of the "Louisiana Wildcats." He was at once summoned into the cabin, and after the object of the proposed expedition had been explained to him, Frank inquired: "Now, Tom, do you want to go with us?" "Douse my to'-gallant top-lights! Yes sir," he replied, eagerly. "But, Cap'n Nelson, I wouldn't like to be left behind, sir, when it comes to the dangerous part of the business, like I was on the night when the paymaster burned that house. I want to go with you to the end, sir, an' if I ever show the white feather, then may I be keelhauled!"

Frank assured him that he would be allowed to accompany them wherever they went, and the coxswain departed satisfied.

When night came, the gig was called away, and Frank, accompanied by the major, Archie, and the coxswain, was set on shore. When the boat had returned to the vessel, which was now in command of the executive officer, the major led his companions through the woods toward the place where the horses were to be obtained. They traveled in silence, following the motions of their guide, who walked along as if he well understood what he was about. The expedition certainly promised better than any in which Frank had before engaged. It was led by a man accustomed to scenes of danger, and was altogether composed of those whose courage and determination had, more than once, been thoroughly tested. They were all well armed, and, in addition to a brace of revolvers, the coxswain carried a heavy saber; for, as he remarked, he might be called upon to "repel boarders," and he wanted some weapon that he knew how to use.

After three or four hours' walk through the woods they came to a fence, where the major paused. Before them was a wide field, in which stood a plantation-house. Bright lights gleamed in the windows, and the major turned to his companions and said:

"There are more people in the house than there were last night."

They all listened intently, and could hear an indistinct murmur of voices, and now and then the tramping of horses in the road that ran in front of the house.

"There are some rebel soldiers in there," continued the major, "and we can now get our horses without any difficulty, already saddled and bridled."

As he spoke, he led the way along the fence toward the road, and they presently came in sight of half a dozen horses which were tied in front of the house. No orders were necessary, for each one knew what was required of him. In a few moments they had quietly secured their horses, and were riding noiselessly down the road. As soon as they were out of sight of the house, they began to make an examination of their prizes, and found that the rebels, who, no doubt, had little dreamed that any one would disturb them there, had left their sabers attached to their saddles, and their pistols in their holsters. Frank and Archie also found themselves possessed, the former of a fine double-barrel shot-gun, loaded with buck-shot, and the latter of a heavy carbine; and the ammunition for each of these weapons had been left on the saddles. The horses were splendid animals, evidently the fruits of a raid upon some well-stocked barn-yard, for they appeared fresh and vigorous, and had undoubtedly been accustomed to the best of care. As soon as they were out of hearing of the people in the house, they put their horses into a gallop, and as the road was excellent, they made rapid headway. For hour after hour they kept on, stopping only now and then to water their horses. Just before daylight the major, who had scarcely spoken during the whole ride, suddenly came to a halt. As his companions gathered about him, he said, almost in a whisper: "Now, boys, we are at our journey's end. There's the house!" and as he spoke, he pointed to a large building just ahead of them. "My advice, captain," he continued, turning to Frank, "would be to ride carefully up in front of the house, hitch our horses - for of course, we must not lose them - and then burst open the door and gobble up the guerrilla before he has time to get out of bed."

This plan was adopted. Riding noiselessly up to the gate, they dismounted, and after tying their horses, they drew their sabers (as it was their intention to rely entirely upon the *sight* of these weapons to bring the guerrilla to terms). Then they entered the yard, and ascended the steps that led on to a wide portico. Here the major, who was in advance, paused a moment, to see that his companions were close behind him, and then, placing his shoulder against the door, with one strong push, forced it open. They all sprang into the house, Frank and Archie being close beside the major, and found themselves, to their utter astonishment, in the presence of a dozen guerrillas, who started from their blankets in alarm. So great was their surprise, that both parties for an instant stood gazing at each other, as if suddenly deprived of the power of action.

"Sink my tarry wig, Cap'n Nelson, but here's a scrape for

honest men to be in!" exclaimed the coxswain, who had kept as close to his officer as possible. "Here *is* a scrape!"

Their position was not an enviable one. There they were, forty miles from their vessel, almost in the heart of an enemy's country, and confronted by three times their number of armed rebels, who, no doubt, could be speedily reinforced. It was too late to retreat, even had they felt disposed to do so. But the idea never once entered their heads. So intent were they upon the capture of the guerrilla chief, that they thought of nothing else, and they were perfectly well aware that the only way to get out of the house was to fight their way through their enemies.

The period of inaction lasted only for an instant; then a few of the rebels, springing to their feet, retreated precipitately through the back door; but the others, recovering from their surprise, and comprehending the nature of the attack, bravely stood their ground, and one tall fellow sprang forward and struck savagely at the major with his sword. But the scout was on the alert, receiving the blow upon his own saber, and before the rebel had time to renew his attack, a shot from a revolver stretched him lifeless on the floor.

This opened the fight. The example of the rebel was quickly followed by his comrades, who, depending wholly upon their sabers, rushed upon the officers with the utmost fury. But they were bravely met. The latter stubbornly held their ground, and parrying the blows directed at them, used their revolvers with deadly effect. At this moment a door at the further end of the hall suddenly opened, and a man sprang out, carrying a short, heavy sword.

"Give it to 'em, lads!" he shouted, hurrying forward to join in the fight. "Give it to 'em. No quarter to the Yankees!"

This was the guerrilla chief, and the order he had just given told Frank and his companions, in plain language, that if overpowered, no mercy would be shown them.

The rebels, encouraged by the voice of their leader, redoubled the fury of their attacks, and the officers were driven to the wall. The coxswain, on entering, had closed the door to prevent the escape of the guerrilla, and thus their retreat was cut off; but they had the advantage of position, for the rebels, unable to get behind them, must make their attacks in front. Already had their ranks been thinned by the fire of the revolvers, but those who had at first retreated now began to return and take the places of those who had been shot down. At last Frank's revolver was empty. He had another in his pocket, but could not get an opportunity to draw it. He must now depend upon his saber. Grasping it with both hands, he bravely met the attack of the leader of the guerrillas, who had succeeded in working his way in front of him. The latter's heavy sword descended with terrible force. Frank's guard was broken down, and he was sent reeling to the floor. The rebel again raised his sword, and, as Frank was entirely unarmed, he gave himself up for lost. One thought of home, of his mother and sister, flashed through his mind, and then he saw the bright blade swiftly descending. It was met, however, by the coxswain, who seeing the danger of his officer, interposed his own sword, and turned the rebel's weapon aside. Frank was on his feet again in an instant, and seeing a musket, with a bayonet attached, standing in the corner, he seized it with a shout of joy. If there was any thing he thoroughly understood, it was the bayonet-exercise. He remembered that the knowledge of it had once saved his life, and he had never let an opportunity to perfect himself in it pass unimproved. He now felt safe; and seeing the coxswain gradually retreating before the furious attacks of the guerrilla chief, he sprang forward, and with one blow sent the sword flying from his hand and bore him to the floor. This move was seconded by Archie, who sprang to his cousin's side with a revolver in each hand, firing right and left among the rebels, who, dismayed at the fall of their leader, began to retreat. But so closely were they followed, that escape was impossible. The chief, after trying in vain to regain his feet, and seeing the bayonet pointed straight at his breast, shouted most lustily for quarter.

"Surrender!" shouted the major. "Throw down your arms!"

The rebels having lost more than half of their number, and knowing the deadly effects of the revolvers which were aimed at their heads, gladly complied, and the fight was at an end.

Although Frank and his companions had heard the order, "No quarter to the Yankees!" the thought of taking vengeance upon those who, had they been the victors, would have shown no mercy, never once entered their heads - they were more humane.

With the surrender of the rebels the object of the expedition had been accomplished - the guerrilla chief was their prisoner!

CHAPTER XIII

TOM THE COXSWAIN

Now that the excitement was over, and Frank began to think more calmly, he found that he was wounded. The blow which had broken down his guard had spent its force on his head, which was bleeding profusely from a long, ragged cut. His face and clothing were covered with blood, but the wound had caused him no inconvenience. After Archie had bandaged it with his handkerchief, Frank began to look about him. The force of the rebels had originally consisted of fifteen men, of whom eight were lying, either dead or wounded, upon the floor. He could scarcely believe his eyes, and wondered how he and his companions had ever secured a victory against such heavy odds. Had the rebels, instead of relying upon their sabers and the superiority of their numbers, made use of the firearms that during the fight had become scattered about the hall, the result would have been far different. The fight, although a most severe one while it lasted, was not of more than five minutes' duration, and during that time eight rebels had been disabled, and six captured by four determined men; one only had escaped. As Archie afterward said, in a letter to his father, "It was the biggest *little* fight" he was ever engaged in.

"Now, boys," said the major, as soon as he had satisfied himself that the remaining rebels were disarmed, "we've no time to lose. Paymaster, you and the coxswain station yourselves in those doors, and keep a good look-out, to prevent surprise. Captain, we will secure these prisoners."

One of the blankets that lay on the floor was speedily cut into strips, and with these the rebels, one after the other, were bound hand and foot. While this was going on, the leader of the guerrillas stood leaning against the wall, no doubt looking into the future, and pondering upon the punishment which, according to his own barbarous mode of warfare, he was certain would be meted out to him. He well knew what course *he* would have pursued, had he been the victor instead of the prisoner, and, judging his captors by himself, he fully expected a speedy and terrible vengeance to be taken upon him. As these thoughts passed through his mind, he determined to make one bold effort at escape. Hastily glancing toward the door, where Archie stood looking up and down the road, he suddenly sprang forward, and giving him a violent push, that sent him headlong upon the portico, he jumped down the steps, and started for the gate at the top of his speed; but before he had gone half the distance, he was overtaken by the coxswain and thrown to the ground. The sailor, instead of standing in the door, in his eagerness, as he expressed it, to "ketch the first glimpse of any guerrilla craft that might be sailin' about," had come round to the front of the house just as the rebel had made his attempt to escape. Archie sprang to his feet and ran to the assistance of the coxswain, and by the time Frank and the major arrived, the rebel, who struggled most desperately, had been overpowered, and his hands bound behind his back. In a few moments more the prisoners were all secured, and, after a horse had been caught and saddled, the guerrilla placed upon it, his hands still bound, and the coxswain was ordered to take charge of him. The dead and wounded, together with the other prisoners, were left in the house, the doors of which were closed and fastened. They would, no doubt, soon be relieved by their friends, for the rebel who had escaped would, of course, procure assistance as soon as possible.

As soon as the major had satisfied himself that every thing was ready for the start, he mounted his horse and led the way down the road. It was now broad daylight, and their first thought was to place a safe distance between themselves and the scene of the fight, and then halt in the woods until night, when they would return to the vessel. But if this plan was adopted, it would give the guerrillas, who, of course, would hasten to the rescue of their leader, time to get between them and the river, in which case their capture was certain. Frank, who believed that every instant of time was valuable, and who delighted in dashing exploits, was in favor of returning at once to the vessel. Their horses were comparatively fresh, and, if they rode rapidly, they could make good their retreat before a sufficient force could be collected to pursue them. The major and Frank talked over these different plans as they rode along side by side, and the latter course was finally adopted. It was at once communicated to the others, and they pushed forward with all possible speed. Frank and the major rode in front, followed by the coxswain, who held fast to the horse which their prisoner rode, and Archie brought up the rear. In this manner they dashed along, passing several plantation-houses, whose inmates ran to the doors and gazed at them in astonishment. Half a dozen miles were passed over in this way without stopping, except to water their horses, and without seeing a single armed rebel, and Frank began to hope that the dangerous part of the undertaking was passed. If attacked by a superior force, the chances were that they would not only lose their prisoner, whose capture had been effected in so gallant a manner, but also their own liberty, and the thought of the treatment they would receive, judging by the order the guerrilla chief had given his men at the commencement of the fight, was enough to nerve them to make the greatest exertions to effect their escape. They had reloaded their pistols, the effective use of which had gained them a victory over almost four times their number, and Frank and Archie carried the shot-gun and carbine which they had found attached to the saddles of their horses, ready for instant use.

The rapid pace at which they were traveling had, at the end of an hour, put half a dozen miles more between them and the house where the fight had taken place, and they began to hope that, if they were followed at all, they were leaving the enemy behind. At length they came to a place where the road ran through a deep ravine, the sides of which were thickly covered with trees and bushes. They dashed along, their horses hoofs ringing loud and clear on the hard road, but as they came suddenly around a bend, almost before they were aware of it, they had run into the very midst of a small band of rebels, who were traveling as rapidly as themselves. They were not entirely unprepared for this encounter. Although they had hoped that they might be able to avoid it, they had held themselves in readiness for it, while the rebels, being taken by surprise, scattered in every direction, as if fully expecting to see a whole army of Federals close at their heels. As they dashed by, Frank fired both barrels of his gun, which emptied more than one saddle, and the others had just time to follow with a volley from their revolvers, when another bend in the road hid them from sight. It was quickly done. Before the rebels had time to think twice, the danger was over. The enemy had met them, sent three of their number to the ground, and disappeared as rapidly as they had come. But the rebels did not remain long inactive. They quickly satisfied themselves that those who had just passed were not the advance-guard of an army, as they had at first supposed, and presently the officers heard the clatter of hoofs behind them, accompanied with loud yells, and knew that the guerrillas had commenced the pursuit. Although, as we have said, the rebels had but a small force, they still greatly outnumbered Frank's party, and nothing but the most rapid flight could save them. Frank's only fear was that their pursuers would come in sight of them, and begin to pick them off at long range with their carbines, a proceeding which nothing but the numerous windings in the road prevented.

"If we do not get into a scrimmage, boys," said the major, speaking as calmly as though he was at that very moment safe in the cabin of the Boxer, "we must stick together, if possible; but if they come on us in a heavy force, we must separate and every man take care of himself."

"Oh, you needn't look so mighty pleased, Johnny!" exclaimed the coxswain, addressing himself to his prisoner, who now looking upon his rescue as beyond a doubt, could not repress a smile of triumph. "Shiver my timbers! you're not loose yet.

You're just as safe here as though you were in the brig [Footnote: The brig is a small dark apartment in the hold of a vessel, in which culprits are confined.] and in double irons. Look as mad as you please, Johnny," he continued, as the guerrilla scowled savagely upon him, "a man who has smelt powder in a'most every battle fought on the Mississippi River an't often skeered by looks."

The major had, several times during the retreat, cautioned the coxswain to keep a fast hold of his prisoner, and not to allow him to escape under any circumstances. But Frank, who knew his man, had never thought the caution necessary. He had often seen the sailor in action on board ship, and the gallant manner in which he had saved his officer's life during the fight at the house, had fully satisfied the young commander that the coxswain was not the man to shrink from his duty because it was dangerous. His reply to the major had been:

"If this Johnny rebel an't safe in the brig tonight, sir, then Captain Nelson will have to make a new cox'son for the first cutter, an' another cap'n for that number two gun. I'll either take him safe through, or I'll never hear the bo'son pipe to dinner ag'in."

All this while they had been tearing along the road as fast as their horses could carry them, but rapidly as they went, the sounds of pursuit grew louder, and the yells fiercer and more distinct, showing that the guerrillas were gaining on them. Suddenly they emerged from the woods, and found before them a long, straight road, with broad fields on each side. Before they could pass this, the rebels would certainly come in sight, and, if they did not overtake them, they would at least open fire on them with their carbines.

Frank gradually drew in his horse and fell back beside his cousin. Archie was deadly pale, but he sat firmly on his horse and handled his carbine with a steady hand.

"Archie," said he, "you and I must cover the retreat of the

others. Don't waste your ammunition now."

They had accomplished perhaps a quarter of the distance across the road when the foremost of their pursuers came in sight. In an instant Archie turned in his saddle, and leaving his horse to pick out his own road, he raised his gun to his shoulder and fired. A moment afterward a riderless horse was rearing and plunging about among the rebels, throwing them into confusion. This was the time for Frank, and he discharged both barrels of his gun in quick succession. The buckshot must have done terrible execution, for when the smoke cleared away, they saw the rebels retreating to the cover of the bushes. One, more daring than the rest, lingered a moment, to fire his carbine, and the fugitives heard the bullet sing through the air above their heads.

Although they were not more than five minutes crossing the road and entering the woods on the opposite side, it seemed an age to them, and they had scarcely reached the cover of the trees, when the rebels again coming in sight, fired a scattering volley after them, which rattled through the trees and sent a shower of leaves and twigs about them. The guerrillas then continued the pursuit as fiercely as ever, every time they came in sight firing their carbines, which Archie answered with effect; but they wisely kept out of range of the buck-shot in Frank's double-barrel.

Hour after hour the chase continued, the guerrillas every time they appeared having their ranks thinned by Archie's unerring rifle, until finally the fugitives heard a sound that told them in plain language that their danger was yet by no means passed. A whole chorus of hoarse yells arose from the depths of the woods, showing that their pursuers had received heavy reinforcements, and were urging forward their horses to overtake them, But the river was not more than two miles distant, and as the rebels were fully a quarter of a mile behind, they were confident they would yet escape, if their horses could hold out fifteen minutes longer. For some time past this had been their only fear. The rapid pace was telling on the animals severely, and Frank's horse especially began to show signs of distress, the young commander having several times been obliged to use the point of his saber to compel him to keep pace with the others. The rebels gained rapidly, and presently, just as the fugitives emerged from the woods, in full view of the river, they could hear the tramping of their horses behind them. Before them was a clear space of fully a mile in extent, that must be crossed before they reached the river, and their pursuers might overtake and capture them within sight of their vessel. Presently several men were seen running about on the deck of the Boxer, and then a puff of smoke arose from one of the ports, and a shell went shrieking over their heads and burst in the woods.

The crew of the vessel, in obedience to Frank's orders, had kept a good look-out for them, and hearing the yells of the pursuing rebels, had at once opened fire. When the smoke cleared away, Frank saw the crew of the gig hurrying to their places. The boat was lowered into the water, and pulled rapidly toward the shore. If they could but reach the bank of the river they would be safe. At this moment the rebels appeared in sight, and a volley from their carbines sent the bullets about the fugitives like hail-stones. Frank turned in his saddle and fired one barrel of his gun among them, and was about to give them the contents of the other, when his horse stumbled and fell, throwing him at full length on the ground. Frank had been expecting this, and for the last half hour had ridden with his feet out of the stirrups, so that in case the accident did happen, he would not be entangled in the saddle. As it was, he was thrown some distance in advance of the horse, which, too exhausted to rise, lay panting on the ground. Frank, however, instantly recovered his feet, and was about to start after his companions, when he saw the coxswain, with a knife in his hand, working desperately to free himself from the saddle of his own fallen horse. Frank at once sprang to his assistance, and catching the knife from his hand, severed the strap that confined him, and set him at liberty. The coxswain, as soon as he had regained his feet, ran up to the horse which the prisoner rode, and which had stopped the moment the sailor fell, and pulling the guerrilla from the saddle, lifted him in his arms as though he had been an infant, and ran toward the boat. The rebels by this time were within easy rifle-range, and in spite of the shells that burst about them, seemed determined to effect the release of their leader, until one more accurately aimed than the others, exploded in their very midst, cutting down horses and riders with terrible slaughter; another and another followed, and when Frank and his companions stepped into the gig, the rebels were in full retreat. When they arrived on board the vessel, the coxswain delivered his prisoner to the master-at-arms, who ironed him, and lodged him safely in the brig.

Their long ride had taxed their endurance to the utmost; but, by the next day, they had fully recovered from their fatigue, and shortly after dinner Frank ordered the officer of the deck to have all hands mustered. The crew speedily assembled on the quarter-deck, and among them stood the coxswain, who, at a motion from Frank, stepped out from among his companions, holding his cap in his hand, and looking altogether like a man who expected "a good blowing up" for some grievous offense. But he soon found that he was not to be reprimanded, for, to his utter astonishment, Frank proceeded to give the officers and crew a full account of the fight at the house, speaking in the highest terms of the old sailor's bravery. He then addressed the coxswain, saying:

"Now, Tom, what can I do for you? What do you want? Would you like a leave of absence, to go home and visit your friends?"

"Avast heavin' there, Cap'n Nelson, if you please!" answered the coxswain, hastily. "I was brought up on board a man-o'-war, sir," he continued, whirling his cap in his hand, "an' have follered the sea for goin' nigh on to thirty-five year, but this is the first time I ever had my cap'n say, 'Thank ye, Tom,' to me for doin' my duty. I an't the only chap, sir, that wouldn't see harm come to you. There's many a man in this crew that would have done the same thing, at the risk of his own life. As for home an' friends, sir, I have none. But, cap'n, there's one favor I have thought of askin' you for. There's no gunner's-mate on board this vessel, an' I think I can take charge of the magazine - don't you, sir?"

This was a small reward for a man to ask of the captain, who would gladly have granted him any favor in his power; but promotion on board ship, among the men, is given only to the most deserving, and the old sailor made this request with a timidity he had never shown before an enemy; and even after he had made it, he regarded his officer as though he fully expected a refusal. But Frank, who could scarcely refrain from smiling at the man's earnest manner, turned to Archie and said:

"Paymaster, please rate Thomas Willis on your books as gunner's-mate from the time the other mate was discharged."

This was something more than the coxswain had expected. The former gunner's-mate had been discharged from the service nearly two months before, and this gave the old sailor a considerable amount of back pay. Frank had delayed the appointment of a gunner's-mate, not because he did not need one, but because there were many good men among his crew, and he wished to give the appointment to the most deserving, and thus make promotion something worth working for. Frank then dismissed the men, who returned to the lower deck, fully satisfied in their own minds that "Cap'n Nelson was the best man any crew ever sailed under."

CHAPTER XIV

A REBEL TRICK

The next day Frank and the major made out their reports of the expedition. The former's, as usual, was short and to the point, conveying, in a few lines, the information that their object had been accomplished. He described the fight in the house as a "short skirmish," and made it appear that their success was owing to the gallant behavior of the major, Archie, and the coxswain. In fact, one, to have read the report, would have supposed that Frank had been merely a looker-on, instead of one of the principal actors. But the major went more into details, and the part Frank had taken in the fight was described in glowing language, and his bravery highly complimented. While thus engaged, the orderly entered the cabin and reported a small party of rebels approaching with a flag of truce. Frank went on deck, and saw several men galloping toward the vessel, waving a white flag, to attract their attention. When they reached the top of the bank, they dismounted from their horses, and appeared to be waiting for some one to come ashore.

For some moments, Frank was undecided how to act. He remembered that he had once been sent on shore with a flag of truce which had not been respected, he having been detained a prisoner, and he did not like the idea of receiving a white flag from men whom he knew would not respect it themselves; besides, he had received no orders in regard to communicating with the rebels, and he did not know whether he had a right to do so or not.

"Well, major, what do you think of this, sir?" he asked, turning toward the scout, who stood close at his side.

"It's a trick of some kind, captain," replied the latter. "Depend upon it, it's a trick."

"If that is so," said Frank, "I will try and find out what it is." Then, raising his voice, he called out, "What do you want out there?"

"I want to come on board," shouted one of the rebels, in reply. "I want to see the captain."

"Well, speak out; you can't come on board. What do you want?"

The rebels consulted together for a few moments, and then one of them replied:

"We have a Yankee prisoner, and want to exchange him for Captain Thorne. If you will let one of us come on board, perhaps we can make some arrangements with you."

"You can't come on board," shouted Frank, "that's settled. But where's your prisoner?"

"Out in the woods, under guard."

"They've got no prisoner, captain," said the major. "All they want is to see the inside of your vessel, and find out how many men and guns you have."

"Well, they'll have to go away without accomplishing their object," said Frank. "I can't make any arrangements for an exchange," he shouted, "until I see your prisoner."

The rebels lingered a moment, as if in consultation, and then mounted their horses and rode away. Every one who had heard the conversation laughed at the idea of attempting to deceive Captain Nelson with so shallow a trick, and the circumstance was soon forgotten by all except Frank, who knew that the guerrillas would not abandon their project simply because their first attempt had failed. Although he made no remark, he resolved to be doubly vigilant, and to be ready for any emergency.

Two days afterward the dispatch-boat came alongside, on her way up the river, and the major took passage on her for Cairo.

"I'm sorry to be obliged to leave you, captain," said he, as he stood ready to start, "for, if I am not very much mistaken, you'll have lively times here before long. The rebels are up to something, depend upon it. Don't let them catch you off your guard. Good luck to you!"

It was lonesome in the cabin after the major left, for he was a good companion, and both Frank and Archie had become very much attached to him.

The dispatch-boat had scarcely left the Boxer, when the officer of the deck reported a canoe approaching. It came from up the river, and, by the aid of the spy-glass, they discovered that it contained two men and was loaded with vegetables. It was customary for gun-boats to purchase such provisions as they needed from the people who lived along the banks, and in some places market-boats were received regularly every day. The men were paid, either in money, or, as they generally preferred, in coffee, flour, or sugar, from the paymaster's store-rooms; but this was the first time the Boxer had ever been visited, and this circumstance, taken in connection with the flag of truce, made Frank suspicious.

"Shall we allow them to come alongside, sir?" asked the officer of the deck.

"Yes," replied Frank, who had already determined upon his

plans, "allow them to come on board, if they wish to do so;" and here he gave the officer a few rapid orders, which the latter hurried below to execute. The Boxer had a full crew of sixty-five men, who were in an admirable state of discipline; but Frank had sent the officer below to order the most of the men into the hold, out of sight, and to remove the small arms about the deck. The major's warning was still ringing in his ears, and the young commander could not rid himself of the impression that the market men who were now approaching were in some way connected with guerrillas. If it was a trick, he resolved to help it along. As the boat approached, it was hailed by the sentinel on the fore-castle, who asked the men their business, and was informed that they had "garden truck" which they wanted to "swap for sugar, flour, an' sich like."

The men were then permitted to come alongside, and one of them was at once conducted into the cabin, where a bargain was soon concluded, Frank agreeing to take the whole boatload of vegetables, and to give the man two pounds of flour, three pounds of sugar, and six pounds of coffee. The young commander was now fully satisfied that the only object of the men in visiting the vessel was not to dispose of their vegetables, for the man rather overdid his part. He gazed with open mouth at every thing he saw, in regular country style, but it was not natural, most of his wonder, as Archie expressed it, being "put on." The latter went below to order his steward to procure the provisions, and the man inquired -

"Will yer let a feller look about a leetle? This is the fust time I was ever on a gun-boat."

"Certainly," replied Archie, who had received his instructions from Frank; "look about all you please;" and while the steward was weighing the coffee and sugar, he accompanied the man about the vessel. There were not more than a dozen sailors on deck, and most of these appeared to be asleep.

"Be these all the fellers you-uns hev got?" asked the man.

"What's the use of having any more?" replied Archie. "There's no danger here."

"That's so," was the answer; "I haint seed a rebel round for more 'n six months, dog-gone if I hev."

The man walked slowly about the deck, carefully examining every thing he saw, and acting altogether like a backwoodsman who had never seen a gun-boat before. Finally, he said:

"I've heered as how all these 'ere boats hev got hot water; has yourn?"

"Oh, yes, we've got plenty of hot water, but it takes an hour to screw the hose on, so that we can use it."

By this time the provisions were ready, and the market men took their departure, expressing themselves fully satisfied that it wouldn't be a "healthy job" for any rebels to attempt the capture of the Boxer, and promising to be on hand the next day but one with more "garden truck."

As soon as their boat was out of sight, the hatches were raised, the crew poured up out of the hold, and in a short time the Boxer's deck presented its usual appearance of neatness and order. Frank's object had been accomplished, for the market men had gone away satisfied that twenty determined men could easily effect the capture of the gun-boat, and they seemed determined to make the most of what they had seen. Gaines's Landing had been a regular mail station, and the rebels had only been deterred from sending it across the river by the presence of the Boxer. The market men, however, had discovered, as they supposed, that the vessel was but poorly manned, and this being communicated to their leader, (for, as Frank had suspected, they belonged to a regularly-organized band of guerrillas,) the latter determined to dispatch his mail at once.

That night, about ten o'clock, as Frank and Archie sat in the cabin reading, the orderly reported that lights were seen moving about on shore. This was something unusual, and when Frank had watched the light for a moment, he came to the conclusion that the rebels were making some movements, the nature of which he was, of course, unable to determine; but he resolved, if possible, to find out what was going on, and turning to the officer of the deck, ordered the cutter to be called away and furnished with an armed crew. This order was speedily and quietly executed, and when the boat was ready, Frank and his cousin stepped into it, and were pulled noiselessly up the river. The place where the light shone was about half a mile from the vessel, and when they came opposite to it, the crew rested on their oars, giving only an occasional stroke to keep the cutter from floating down the stream, and waited impatiently for the rebels to show themselves.

The light, which gleamed from the shore opposite to the town, seemed to come from a dark lantern, for it would blaze up brightly for a moment, and then disappear. Presently an answering light was shown from the shore nearest to them, when Archie whispered -

"There's a boat coming!"

Frank listened, and could hear the slow, measured strokes of oars, which grew louder and louder as the boat approached. It seemed to be heading directly toward them, and in a few moments more it could be dimly seen, moving through the darkness.

"Give way together!" commanded Frank, and the cutter, propelled by twelve oars, shot alongside the approaching boat, and the sailors seized the gunwale and held her fast. Resistance was useless. Three rebels quietly delivered up their weapons, and one large, well-filled mail-bag was stowed away under the stern sheets of the cutter. The prisoners were taken on board the Boxer, and delivered into the charge of the master-at-arms, while their boat, a leaky affair, requiring constant bailing to keep it afloat, was unceremoniously allowed to sink. The light on the opposite shore was still shown, now at shorter intervals, as if the persons who were managing it had begun to grow impatient. This was the source of much merriment among the sailors, who hoped the "rebels would not grow tired of waiting for their mail."

The next day the Manhattan again came up the river, and, as she approached, made signals for Frank to go on board of her. The gig was called away, and taking the reports of the expedition the young officer and his prisoners shortly stood in the presence of Captain Wilson, who, as soon as he had secured the prisoners, conducted Frank into the cabin. The latter, after presenting his reports, proceeded to give the captain a history of the expedition which had resulted in the capture of the guerrilla chief, of the interview with the flag of truce, and of the manner in which he had deceived the market men and captured the mail, upon hearing which the captain sprang from his chair, and giving Frank a hearty slap on the back, exclaimed:

"Well done, sir! well done! Then you are not entirely unprepared to hear what I have to tell you. I picked up a runaway darkey yesterday, who informs me that the rebels are making preparations to capture the Boxer!"

"I knew something was going on, sir," replied Frank, "and if that is what they are up to, they will not find me unprepared."

"Well, that is what they intend to do. They have been building two large boats, into which they are going to put a sufficient force to overpower you. The attempt is to be made on Wednesday night. Of course, they hope to be able to take you by surprise. This contraband I picked up says he worked on the boats, and that they will hold about forty men each. I shall not be far off when the fight takes place, although I do not suppose you will need any assistance."

The two officers then began an examination of the mail, in

hopes it would throw some further light upon the movements of the guerrillas; but most of the letters were unofficial, and not a word was said about the proposed attempt to capture the Boxer.

At the end of an hour, Frank returned on board his vessel, and the Manhattan steamed down the river toward her station.

CHAPTER XV

HONORABLY DISCHARGED

When Frank reached the Boxer, he sent for the executive officer, told him of what he had heard, and also laid before him the plans he had adopted to defeat the rebels, which met the hearty approval of that gentleman. Frank did not think it best to delay putting the vessel in a state of defense, for the rebels might make the attempt at any time; so he instructed the executive officer to see that the men were kept under cover, so that the rebels, if any were on the watch, might not be able to judge of their numbers. When hammocks were piped that night, not more than a dozen men answered the call, and when bedtime came, the sailors stretched themselves out on deck, ready to take their posts at a moment's warning. The guns were all carefully loaded, the hot-water hose got ready for use, and the anchor fixed so that it could be slipped in an instant. Outside, the appearance of the vessel was not changed, the only thing noticeable being the quantity of smoke that came out of her chimneys. At eight o'clock Frank inspected the boat, and after seeing that every man was in his place, he lay down on the sofa in the cabin, without removing his clothes, and fell asleep. When he awoke, he arose and went on deck, just as the ship's bell was striking midnight. It was very dark, and the only sound that broke the stillness was the splashing of the wheels of a steamer as she went on her way up the river. For an hour he remained on deck, listening, but without hearing any thing suspicious until just as he was about to return to the cabin. He had started down the stairs, when he heard a slight splashing ahead of the vessel, like a heavy oar dipped carefully into the water. He listened a moment, and the sound was repeated.

"There they are! They're coming, sure!" said Archie, who stood at his cousin's side.

"Yes, sir," said Tom, the gunner's-mate, who, in his eagerness to be the first to announce the approach of the rebels, had remained on deck during the whole night. "That's them, sir!"

"Tell the officer of the deck to call all hands to quarters as quietly as possible," said Frank.

The officer ran below, and the young commander heard the sound again, still faint, but nearer and more distinct than the others. It was well that he had not put off his preparations to receive the rebels, for they were certainly approaching. Presently the pilots came up and took their stations at the wheel, and a moment afterward the executive officer came up and reported the crew ready for action. So quietly had the men been aroused, that Frank had not heard them as they moved to their stations. Nearer and nearer came the sound of oars, and suddenly a large flatboat, crowded with men, loomed up through the darkness.

"On deck, there!" whispered Frank, leaning over the rail and speaking to a sailor on the forecastle. "Slip that anchor."

There was the rattling of a chain as this order was executed, and as the man sprang through one of the ports, a sheet of flame covered the forecastle, and two twenty-four pound shells went crashing and shrieking among the rebels.

The pilots rang the bell for the engineers to "come ahead," and as the Boxer turned out into the river, thus bringing her broadside guns to bear on the boat, two more shells completed the ruin. The rebels were caught in their own trap. Their boat was sinking, half their number either dead or wounded, and all who were able to swim were springing into the water and making for the nearest shore.

It was so dark Frank could not see the havoc that had been made among the guerrillas, and he was about to give them another broadside, when he heard loud cries for quarter. That boat was disposed of, and he turned to look for the other, (for Captain Wilson had said there were two of them,) but it was not to be seen. As he afterward learned, the guerrillas, having been completely deceived as to the force of the Boxer, had crowded sixty men into one boat, thinking that force sufficient to insure an easy victory. After running up the river nearly a mile without seeing any signs of the boat, the Boxer returned to her station, and found the rebel craft hard and fast aground. Her deck was covered with dead and wounded, and Frank at once turned his attention to taking care of the latter. Twenty-three wounded guerrillas were conveyed on board the vessel, and delivered into the charge of the doctor and his steward, together with nearly a dozen prisoners, who, being unable to swim, had not dared to leave the boat. The dead were left where they had fallen. The Boxer then returned to her anchorage, and Frank, feeling safe for the remainder of the night, ordered hammocks to be piped, a command which the sailors gladly obeyed, for their soft mattresses were much more comfortable than the hard deck. By the time every thing had been restored to order, the quarter-master reported the Manhattan approaching. Frank answered her signals, and as she came alongside, Captain Wilson sprang on board.

"How is it, captain?" he inquired, as Frank met him at the gangway. "Mercy!" he exclaimed, as he entered the door and saw the wounded rebels lying in rows on the deck. "Lively while it lasted, wasn't it? How many men have you lost?"

"None, sir," replied Frank. "If the rebels fired a shot at us, I don't know it."

"When I heard the firing," continued the captain, "I was afraid you had neglected to make preparations to receive them, and had got yourself into a bad scrape. But I see you are able to take care of yourself."

The captain then returned on board his vessel, which moved out into the river and came to anchor at a short distance from the Boxer, while Frank retired to his room and fell asleep, well satisfied with his night's work.

Early the next morning, a single rebel appeared on the bank, with a flag of truce, and a boat being sent out from the Manhattan, he was conveyed on board that vessel. In a short time, however, it returned and set the rebel on board the Boxer.

"I want permission to bury our dead," said the guerrilla, on being shown into the cabin.

"You must see Captain Wilson about that," replied Frank. "I have no authority while he is here."

"I have just been to see him," replied the rebel, "and he sent me to you. He says you command this station."

This was a compliment seldom paid a young officer; but the fact was, Captain Wilson was so elated at Frank's success, that he determined to take every opportunity to make his approval known. The young commander, of course, granted the request, and soon after the Manhattan steamed down the river.

About a week afterward, a tin-clad came up, and her captain came on board the Boxer and presented Frank with written orders to report to Captain Wilson without delay.

"I expect," said he, "that you will take my old station. If you do, you will have your hands full, for boats are fired into every day; but, somehow, I was always at the wrong end of my beat to meet the rebels."

When the captain had returned on board his vessel, the Boxer got up steam, and, in obedience to her orders, started down the river. They found Captain Wilson the next day, and Frank was assigned a new station. His beat was about five miles in length, and was a noted place for guerrillas. Steamboat captains dreaded to pass it, for their boats were fired into, and often badly cut up. The rebels had a battery of three guns, with which they were constantly dodging from one point to another, always taking good care, however, to keep out of reach of the gun-boats. On the second day Frank arrived at his station, and while running idly about - for his orders from Captain Wilson were to "keep moving" - a steamer passed them on her way up the river, and Frank ordered the pilot to round-to and follow her. The order was obeyed, but they had not gone more than half a mile, when a battery, mounted on a point which ran for some distance out into the river, opened on the steamer. The Boxer was at that moment behind the point and out of sight of the rebels, who, however, were soon made aware of her presence; for they had scarcely fired two rounds before a shell dismounted one of their guns. Their surprise was complete, and abandoning their battery, they ran into the woods for protection. The Boxer rounded the point, all the while shelling the woods, and Frank, seeing the guns deserted, landed with his vessel and secured them. That guerrilla station was, for the present, broken up. So thought Frank, who ordered the pilot to proceed up the river until he found the Manhattan. The next day the battery was delivered up to Captain Wilson, who sent it by the dispatch-boat to Mound City, which was then the naval station.

From that time hostilities along the river gradually ceased. The Boxer for nearly a year ran from one end of her beat to the other without encountering a single armed rebel. Then came the news of the glorious success of the Army of the Potomac, followed by the intelligence of a general surrender of the rebel forces. The Boxer was dressed with flags, salutes fired, and officers and crew looked forward with impatience to the time when they would be permitted to return home. At length came the long expected order to report to the admiral at Mound City, where the reduction of the squadron was rapidly going on.

Although Frank was impatient to see his quiet little home once more, he was reluctant to part from his crew, whom, upon his arrival at the navy-yard, he had received orders to discharge. One by one the sailors came into the cabin, and the hearty grasp of their hands, and the earnest manner in which they wished their commander "plain sailing through life," showed that their feelings were not unlike his own.

One morning, upon inquiry at the navy-yard post-office, Frank was presented with two official documents, which proved to be leaves of absence for himself and Archie for three months, "At the expiration of that time," so read the document, "if your services, are no longer required, you will he honorably discharged from the navy of the United States. Acknowledge the receipt of this leave, and send your address to the department."

As soon as this order had been complied with, the cousins began to make preparations to start for home. Their trunks had been packed several days before, in readiness for an immediate departure, and in three hours after the receipt of their leaves they had taken their seats in the train bound for Portland. The ride had never seemed so long, nor had the cars ever moved so slowly: but, in due time, they reached the city in safety. Frank remained but one day in Portland, for he was anxious to reach home. The "Julia Burton" still made her regular trips from Augusta to Lawrence, and on the third day he reached the village. Brave was the first to welcome him as he stepped out of the hack that had conveyed him from the wharf to the cottage, and not recognizing his master, muffled up as he was in his heavy overcoat, he stood at the gate, growling savagely, as if to warn him that he had ventured close enough. But one word was sufficient. The faithful animal had not forgotten the sound of the familiar voice, and bounding over the fence, he nearly overpowered his master with caresses.

The meeting with his mother and sister we shall not attempt to describe. Those who have passed through similar scenes can easily imagine that joy reigned supreme in that house.

About a week after his arrival at home, Archie Winters and his parents reached the village, the latter having "taken a holiday" in honor of the young paymaster's safe return. The cousins spent their furlough in visiting their old hunting and fishing-grounds, and in calling upon their friends. George and Harry Butler had returned, the former with an empty sleeve, having lost his arm in the Battle of the Wilderness. But all their companions had not been as fortunate as themselves. More than one had been offered upon the altar of their country, and many a familiar face was missing.

At the expiration of their three months' leave, Frank and Archie received their honorable discharges from the service, the sight of which recalled vividly to their minds many a thrilling scene through which they had passed. How changed the scene now from that when they had first bid adieu to their homes, to join the ranks of their country's defenders! "Then a gigantic rebellion was in progress; armed men sentineled each other from Virginia to the Rio Grande; and the land was filled with the crash of contending armies. Now, the rebel forces are vanquished, their banner in the dust; the slave empire that was to rise upon the ruins of the Republic is itself in ruins; and the soldiers and sailors of the Union, returning their weapons to the arsenals, have exchanged their honored blue for the citizen's garb, and resumed their peaceful avocations, as modest and unassuming as though they had never performed the deeds of valor that have filled the whole civilized world with wonder."

Frank and Archie are proud of the part they have borne in the war of the Rebellion, and will never forget their varied and eventful experience in the MISSISSIPPI SQUADRON.

Choose from Thousands of 1stWorldLibrary Classics By

A. M. Barnard
Ada Leverson
Adolphus William Ward
Aesop
Agatha Christie
Alexander Aaronsohn
Alexander Kielland
Alexandre Dumas
Alfred Gatty
Alfred Ollivant
Alice Duer Miller
Alice Turner Curtis
Alice Dunbar
Ambrose Bierce
Amelia E. Barr
Amory H. Bradford
Andrew Lang
Andrew McFarland Davis
Andy Adams
Anna Sewell
Annie Besant
Annie Hamilton Donnell
Annie Payson Call
Annonaymous
Anton Chekhov
Arnold Bennett
Arthur Conan Doyle
Arthur M. Winfield
Arthur Ransome
Atticus
B.H. Baden-Powell
B. M. Bower
Baroness Emmuska Orczy
Baroness Orczy
Basil King
Bayard Taylor
Ben Macomber
Bertha Muzzy Bower
Bjornstjerne Bjornson
Booth Tarkington
Boyd Cable
Bram Stoker
C. Collodi
C. E. Orr
C. M. Ingleby
Carolyn Wells
Catherine Parr Traill
Charles A. Eastman
Charles Dickens

Charles Dudley Warner
Charles Farrar Browne
Charles Ives
Charles Kingsley
Charles Klein
Charles Amory Beach
Charles Hanson Towne
Charles Lathrop Pack
Charles Whibley
Charles Willing Beale
Charlotte M. Braeme
Charlotte M. Yonge
Charlotte Perkins Stetson
Clair W. Hayes
Clarence Day Jr.
Clarence E. Mulford
Clemence Housman
Confucius
Cornelis DeWitt Wilcox
Cyril Burleigh
D. H. Lawrence
Daniel Defoe
David Garnett
Dinah Craik
Don Carlos Janes
Donald Keyhoe
Dorothy Kilner
Dougan Clark
Douglas Fairbanks
E. Nesbit
E.P.Roe
E. Phillips Oppenheim
Earl Barnes
Edgar Rice Burroughs
Edith Van Dyne
Edith Wharton
Edward J. O'Biren
Edward S. Ellis
Edwin L. Arnold
Eleanor Atkins
Eliot Gregory
Elizabeth Gaskell
Elizabeth McCracken
Elizabeth Von Arnim
Ellem Key
Emerson Hough
Emilie F. Carlen
Emily Dickinson
Enid Bagnold

Enilor Macartney Lane
Erasmus W. Jones
Ernie Howard Pie
Ethel Turner
Ethel Watts Mumford
Eugenie Foa
Eugene Wood
Eustace Hale Ball
Evelyn Everett-green
Everard Cotes
F. H. Cheley
F. J. Cross
Federick Austin Ogg
Ferdinand Ossendowski
Francis Bacon
Francis Darwin
Frances Hodgson Burnett
Frances Parkinson Keyes
Frank Gee Patchin
Frank Harris
Frank Jewett Mather
Frank L. Packard
Frank V. Webster
Frederic Stewart Isham
Frederick Trevor Hill
Frederick Winslow Taylor
Friedrich Kerst
Friedrich Nietzsche
Fyodor Dostoyevsky
G.A. Henty
G.K. Chesterton
Gabrielle E. Jackson
Garrett P. Serviss
Gaston Leroux
George A. Warren
George Ade
Geroge Bernard Shaw
George Durston
George Ebers
George Eliot
George Gissing
George MacDonald
George Meredith
George Orwell
George Sylvester Viereck
George Tucker
George W. Cable
George Wharton James
Gertrude Atherton

Grace E. King
Grace Gallatin
Grant Allen
Guillermo A. Sherwell
Gulielma Zollinger
Gustav Flaubert
H. A. Cody
H. B. Irving
H.C. Bailey
H. G. Wells
H. H. Munro
H. Irving Hancock
H. Rider Haggard
H. W. C. Davis
Hamilton Wright Mabie
Hans Christian Andersen
Harold Avery
Harold McGrath
Harriet Beecher Stowe
Harry Houidini
Helent Hunt Jackson
Helen Nicolay
Hendrik Conscience
Hendy David Thoreau
Henri Barbusse
Henrik Ibsen
Henry Adams
Henry Ford
Henry Frost
Henry James
Henry Jones Ford
Henry Seton Merriman
Henry W Longfellow
Herbert A. Giles
Herbert N. Casson
Herman Hesse
Homer
Honore De Balzac
Horace Walpole
Horatio Alger Jr.
Howard Pyle
Howard R. Garis
Hugh Lofting
Hugh Walpole
Humphry Ward
Ian Maclaren
Inez Haynes Gillmore
Irving Bacheller
Israel Abrahams
Ivan Turgenev
J.G.Austin

J. Henri Fabre
J. M. Barrie
J. Macdonald Oxley
J. S. Fletcher
J. S. Knowles
J. Storer Clouston
Jack London
Jacob Abbott
James Allen
James Andrews
James Baldwin
James DeMille
James Joyce
James Lane Allen
James Lane Allen
James Oliver Curwood
James Oppenheim
James Otis
James R. Driscoll
Jane Austen
Janet Aldridge
Jens Peter Jacobsen
Jerome K. Jerome
John Burroughs
John Cournos
John F. Kennedy
John Gay
John Glasworthy
John Habberton
John Joy Bell
John Kendrick Bangs
John Milton
John Philip Sousa
Jonas Lauritz Idemil Lie
Jonathan Swift
Joseph A. Altsheler
Joseph Carey
Joseph Conrad
Joseph E. Badger Jr
Joseph Hergesheimer
Joseph Jacobs
Jules Vernes
Julian Hawthrone
Julie A Lippmann
Justin Huntly McCarthy
Kakuzo Okakura
Kenneth Grahame
Kenneth McGaffey
Kate Langley Bosher
Kate Langley Bosher
Katherine Cecil Thurston

Katherine Stokes
L. A. Abbot
L. T. Meade
L. Frank Baum
Latta Griswold
Laura Lee Hope
Laurence Housman
Lawrence Beasley
Leo Tolstoy
Leonid Andreyev
Lewis Carroll
Lewis Sperry Chafer
Lilian Bell
Lloyd Osbourne
Louis Hughes
Louis Tracy
Louisa May Alcott
Lucy Fitch Perkins
Lucy Maud Montgomery
Lydia Miller Middleton
Lyndon Orr
M. Corvus
M. H. Adams
Margaret E. Sangster
Margaret Vandercook
Margret Penrose
Maria Edgeworth
Maria Thompson Daviess
Mariano Azuela
Marion Polk Angellotti
Mark Overton
Mark Twain
Mary Austin
Mary Catherine Crowley
Mary Cole
Mary Hastings Bradley
Mary Roberts Rinehart
Mary Rowlandson
M. Wollstonecraft Shelley
Maud Lindsay
Max Beerbohm
Myra Kelly
Nathaniel Hawthrone
Nicolo Machiavelli
O. F. Walton
Oscar Wilde
Owen Johnson
P.G. Wodehouse
Paul and Mabel Thorne
Paul G. Tomlinson
Paul Severing

Percy Brebner
Peter B. Kyne
Plato
R. Derby Holmes
R. L. Stevenson
R. S. Ball
Rabindranath Tagore
Rahul Alvares
Ralph Bonehill
Ralph Henry Barbour
Ralph Victor
Ralph Waldo Emmerson
Rene Descartes
Rex Beach
Rex E. Beach
Richard Harding Davis
Richard Jefferies
Richard Le Gallienne
Robert Barr
Robert Frost
Robert Gordon Anderson
Robert L. Drake
Robert Lansing
Robert Lynd
Robert Michael Ballantyne
Robert W. Chambers
Rosa Nouchette Carey
Rudyard Kipling
Samuel B. Allison

Samuel Hopkins Adams
Sarah Bernhardt
Sarah C. Hallowell
Selma Lagerlof
Sherwood Anderson
Sigmund Freud
Standish O'Grady
Stanley Weyman
Stella Benson
Stephen Crane
Stewart Edward White
Stijn Streuvels
Swami Abhedananda
Swami Parmananda
T. S. Ackland
T. S. Arthur
The Princess Der Ling
Thomas A. Janvier
Thomas A Kempis
Thomas Anderton
Thomas Bailey Aldrich
Thomas Bulfinch
Thomas De Quincey
Thomas H. Huxley
Thomas Hardy
Thomas More
Thornton W. Burgess
U. S. Grant
Valentine Williams

Various Authors
Vaughan Kester
Victor Appleton
Virginia Woolf
Walter Camp
Walter Scott
Washington Irving
Wilbur Lawton
Wilkie Collins
Willa Cather
Willard F. Baker
William Dean Howells
William le Queux
W. Makepeace Thackeray
William W. Walter
Winston Churchill
Yei Theodora Ozaki
Yogi Ramacharaka
Young E. Allison
Zane Grey